NIGHT
TERMINUS

NIGHT
TERMINUS

ELLIS SCOTT

RARE
MACHINES

Publisher and acquiring editor: Meghan Macdonald
Cover designer: Laura Boyle
Cover image: Man in train station: Unsplash/Vignesh Moorthy; Gare Toulon, Edouard Baldus ca. 1861; Paper texture: Unsplash/Dan Cristian Padure; Desert: Unsplash/Wolfgang Hasselmann

Library and Archives Canada Cataloguing in Publication

Title: Night terminus / Ellis Scott.
Names: Scott, Ellis, author.
Identifiers: Canadiana (print) 20250238438 | Canadiana (ebook) 20250238454 | ISBN 9781459756151 (softcover) | ISBN 9781459756168 (PDF) | ISBN 9781459756175 (EPUB)
Subjects: LCGFT: Novels.
Classification: LCC PS8637.C686116 N54 2026 | DDC C813/.6—dc23

 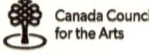 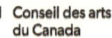 

We acknowledge the support of the Canada Council for the Arts and the Ontario Arts Council for our publishing program. We also acknowledge the financial support of the Government of Ontario, through the Ontario Book Publishing Tax Credit and Ontario Creates, and the Government of Canada.

Care has been taken to trace the ownership of copyright material used in this book. The author and the publisher welcome any information enabling them to rectify any references or credits in subsequent editions.

The publisher is not responsible for websites or their content unless they are owned by the publisher.

Rare Machines, an imprint of Dundurn Press
1382 Queen Street East
Toronto, Ontario, Canada M4L 1C9
dundurn.com, @dundurnpress

for Santosh

If I could figure out a way to remain forever in transition, in the disconnected and unfamiliar, I could remain in a state of perpetual freedom.

— DAVID WOJNAROWICZ, *Close to the Knives: A Memoir of Disintegration*

CHAPTER ONE

LOUIS KOROL

Toward the end of February 1985, after being released from Maudsley Hospital, I took the National Express overnight bus from London Victoria to Dover on my way to France. I snagged a ticket for one pound using my dead friend's coach card, which thankfully had eight months left on it, hoping to catch the 3:00 a.m. Sealink ferry to Calais port and the train from Calais Ville station to disembark in Paris before noon. I had buried seven friends that year and there were still ten months to go.

Well after noon, my train pulled into Gare du Nord station. I slept for most of the journey to Paris, only waking up to the jerking carriage movements as we slowed, and for reasons unknown to me had dreamt of the night before, walking to the ferry terminal from Dover-Pencester coach station. I turned into the briny air of Marine Parade and the floodlights of the ferry dock were to my left, past low-rise blocks of flats that lined the shore of the otherwise characterless promenade and had only gone fifty metres when I came upon a bronze statue of a man on a marble plinth at the centre of a wide, bare lawn. He wore a double-breasted Mariner's coat and tall boots, ready to head off to sea, with a pronounced lean on one leg so that the side of his pelvis dropped below the other, giving him a very provocative bearing. The name on the inscription plate was CHARLES STEWART ROLLS, which rang no bell in my mind. I thought it jaunty that the sculptor had given him white epaulettes, then realized that pigeon droppings covered his shoulders. The smooth, round face, neck forward with intent, stared out over the water from its vantage point at an unseen object or historical event, and I followed its gaze, floating out over an inky sea until I was shaken awake.

A sneaker shoelace had inexplicably come undone as I slumbered. I walked to the exit in the damp air, alighting in no particular hurry, allowing most of the other riders to pass. Looking up at the train shed while walking, admiring the station's fine, decorative skeleton of deep-green wrought-iron pillars that butterflied to meet their girders, I almost ran into a cleaner, head bowed as she swept the platform, wearing a light blue apron uniform over her street clothes. When I apologized in English, she glanced at me, grimaced, and went back to work.

I scouted for a place to sleep later, either near the platforms, which were safest after midnight, or by the departures board in the entrance hall, where it was busiest. One counted on a few dozen backpackers to assemble after dinner and everyone slept close together. Fast-food bags and dirty socks had been left in the corner at the head of the first platform. Empty walls stretched between exit doors to sleep against, just in case, so no one could approach from behind and steal your belongings. The main hall was quiet except for a woman's voice echoing over the loudspeaker, and barren for its cavernous size, save for a small café and boulangerie, a newsstand by a cork noticeboard, and two long, glassed-in counters on both sides of the trellised departures board facing the street entrance. The left sign said BILLETS GRANDES LIGNES in blue neon and the right said RESERVATION INFORMATION in white, both in the same italicized art deco font. A pigeon sprinted for the exit.

As I paced back and forth, scanning the room, I saw a young man sitting motionless as a stone on a bench by the ticket counter near where I stood, hands between his thighs. The stranger stared straight ahead with a downcast expression, lost in thought, wearing a black pea coat and tweed flat cap too big for his head, loose-fitting grey cotton pants, and a burgundy dress shirt open at the collar. His heavy-soled brown boots were tied with striped workers' laces, and he clutched the strap of a large canvas bag. No rings, no necklace.

I approached, turned away, looked around, and walked past him again to take a closer look. He had a boyish face, with full lips, prominent ears, narrow-set eyes, and a wide nose, but with a high bridge and thick, slanted eyebrows, almost Slavic, and dark russet hair peeking out from under his cap.

Unable to read the newsstand headlines, I moved to the noticeboard. A dozen ads for hostels and pensions were pinned to the cork and a few were translated into basic English and Dutch, with tiny maps showing their proximity to the station. I stood there, examining a word in one posting for Pension Normandy around the corner, blanking on the meaning of *chauffage*, cursing my parents for being too cheap to send me to French immersion, when the same stranger appeared beside me, standing very close, perusing the ads. Glancing over, I saw we were the same height, but he had broader shoulders, with pale skin and a line of delicate moles behind his ear, high on his cheeks, and on the crease of his mouth. They gave his face depth, but also innocence, like a baby's that had never seen the sun. I remained still, remembering chauffage meant heating. He turned to me.

"Are you looking for a room for the night?"

"I sure am."

"Oh great, we could find one together to save money, if you're interested."

We exchanged those familiar glances, more than a few beats longer than usual.

"Saving money is always interesting."

"Have you seen anything good, close, and cheap?"

He sounded French. The timbre of his voice was softer and deeper than I imagined, which aged him attractively, and I guessed he was several years older, no more than twenty-five. I pointed to the one with chauffage.

"It means heating."

"It certainly does."

"We won't be cold, anyway, and it's right around the corner."

We introduced ourselves and shook hands. Louis was assured but shy, perhaps not inclined to engage in spontaneous conversations with strangers. Had I refused, I was sure his response would have been a simple nod and polite bow.

We left the station through the swinging doors into traffic, and Louis pulled the brim of his cap down, covering his face. Shafts of sunlight peeked through heavy clouds. He directed me across the street, past the drop-off lane, clutching my elbow and pointing me away from our intended route to avoid passing five gendarmerie standing by the entrance under the monumental stone and glass facade. Surprised by the security, I asked if he knew what was going on.

"Central Paris has been targeted by a series of political bombings, shocking the city. They were very bold, but I didn't expect the police."

Once we had gone twenty metres, he turned us back toward the east pilaster and around the corner, briefly removing his cap to wipe his forehead.

"A Red Army splinter group named Action Directe assassinated a French general in January," he said, "and a few days ago, a Marks and Spencer department store was blown up very close by. People were killed and wounded, and now there are so many armed officers. Even in Brussels-Midi station, there were a lot of police. I saw you admiring the concourse. Is this your first time seeing Gare du Nord?"

"I love old ironworks. I was thinking of where to spend the night because I have little money and need to make it last."

"I'm fine with sleeping outside or eating for free, but not on this trip. So it's good we ran into each other."

Louis glanced behind us as we walked. His most distinguishing trait was his anonymity. He was hard to spot in a crowd, making me question if it was intentional. In a police lineup, he'd be chosen last.

"And yourself? Where are you going and for how long?"

"It's complicated," he said, "but I'm thinking of moving on. I have no agenda and no plans for tomorrow."

We exchanged looks as we walked, but an awkward silence dropped over us and he changed the subject back to trains.

"I have only been to Paris a handful of times before, but my father spoke of Gare du Nord when I was a child. He arrived here as a refugee from East Germany in the 1950s. In a course on European photography at school, I studied the work of Édouard Baldus, who took large-scale panoramic pictures of the French railways. You would like them if you appreciate the station."

"What do they look like?"

"Baldus invented the landmark photograph, leaving out people, allowing the images of the architecture alone to speak for who made them."

"Are you German?"

"No, my father lived in Belorussia, but was Polish, and my mother was Belgian. My parents met after my father was transferred to Belgium, which had more lenient asylum policies for refugees from the East. France had always been sympathetic to communism, which blinded them to what was happening to Poles in the Soviet Union."

Louis looked over his shoulder again.

"But perhaps now," he said, "they will reconsider."

A gust of wind slammed into us as we turned the corner. He pointed to a row of neglected five-storey nineteenth-century buildings beyond a metal fence. We stood on a belvedere parallel to their second floors. When we reached the fence, I saw what must have been the Pension Normandy. On each of the floor's balconies hung signs that said only HOTEL in plain green letters on a white background, giving the Pension Normandy an air of cover. On a moment's notice, because of an indiscretion, it could change the name on the books to Hotel du Lac or Maison Suzanne with no one noticing. Louis looked back one more time as we descended the concrete stairs to a street lined with cars, crossing over to a *tabac* beside the pension. Outside, three men sat smoking in silence around a wooden table, staring lugubriously at the garbage stacked high on the corner. After purchasing wine, hard cheese, bread, and liver pâté at a patisserie next door, we walked back to the Normandy's entrance.

The reception wasn't busy. Indeed, we saw no one except a petite woman with hennaed hair standing behind a curved wooden counter wearing a ribbed, pale green cowl-neck sweater, smoking a cigarette. Louis spoke to her in French. She nodded, and they had a brief conversation. The room was 110 francs, which was very inexpensive. Louis turned and spoke to her again, taking out an identification card from his wallet. She shrugged, flipping her hands back and forth, speaking rapidly as if to a confidante. She took the card and he put his wallet away. The details of my passport were noted in a large, green-covered ledger, and Louis removed a thick bundle of bills from his pocket. I gave him fifty francs and he said that was enough, handing her the money. He smiled at me again and explained that meals here consisted only of breakfast, which was pastry rolls and coffee or tea, served in the pantry along the narrow hall on the ground floor between seven and nine in the morning. The woman handed the key to Louis, who asked her another question. Without responding, she fetched a corkscrew and paring knife from the back room, and we climbed the stairs to the second floor, the floorboards creaking underneath our feet.

The room smelled of smoke, was painted pale green, and lit only by the window, framed by threadbare burgundy curtains. I switched on the overhead light as Louis latched the door twice. To the right of the window, two single beds with curlicue black metal frames and matching nubby chenille cream bedspreads were pushed together. On the side wall, by the beds, hung an aged print of a pastoral scene in a cracked, white plastic frame. To the left, behind a tawdry chintz curtain, a bidet sat next to a bare sink with an exposed drain.

I set my bag on the floor under the window and glanced at the line of cars on the street and the mostly vacant parking lot across the road. A bald man in a black pilot jacket stood by a lamppost near the corner, a motorcycle helmet in his hand, speaking to another man in a leather jacket sitting on an iron bollard. Louis peered out the glass, watching the men, then quickly closed the curtain. He removed his coat, folding it neatly into a square and placing it on the luggage stand in the corner, then untucked his shirt, unbuckling a bulky leather pouch from around his waist and adding the cash from his pocket to a massive wad of bills in the pouch, which he slipped into his bag beside the bed.

"You look unexpectedly nervous," I said.

He shook his head, moved closer, and kissed me.

"I'm probably sick," he said.

Nodding, I kissed him back, and we removed each other's clothes, leaving them scattered at the foot of the bed.

WHEN WE HAD FINISHED, I STRETCHED OUT MY ARMS and licked his bare shoulder, and Louis pulled back the crumpled sheets. There was a small but deep scar near the crown of his head where his hair no longer grew, reminding me of the penultimate scene in *The Omen*, where Gregory Peck finds the devil's birthmark on little Damien's scalp just before he stabs the unholy nanny to death. I got out of bed, walked over to the sink, splashing my face and crotch with water, and pissed into the bidet. Louis got up, smoothed the bottom sheet, checked his bag again, then opened the curtain just a crack and gazed out the window. I opened the wine and cut four slices of cheese, spreading pâté on a chunk of bread, and we both lay back down. As we ate, I inspected the shabby print on the wall, Cézanne's *Mont Sainte-Victoire*, but the colours had faded so much the painting now resembled any vague pasture and mountain in Europe, which better suited the room. I slipped my head into the crook of his shoulder and felt his chest muscles slacken.

"Your accent," he said. "American?"

"Canadian," I said. "We immigrated there for almost a decade when I was still young, and I never lost the drawl."

"I always mistake New Zealanders for Australians as well."

"Your English is excellent."

"My father was a linguistics teacher, so encouraged me to study languages. He pulled me out of my home school as a boy and enrolled me for two years in an English immersion school in our town in the Ardennes. Why he didn't choose German was a mystery at first, as my skills needed improvement."

"So why English?"

"It was my father's dream to go to America, like many minorities under occupation in the Soviet Union. The further he could run from Marxism, popular in Northern Europe, the better. I realized later he was just investing in his dream. Partly because of my relationship with him, I sympathized with socialism. It became my revenge."

I reached back and fed him a slice of cheese. A piece dropped onto the sheet, which he picked up at once, clucking his tongue.

"Does your father still live in the Ardennes? What happened in his exile?"

"He's dead. My mother as well. About his escape across Eastern Europe, I only know parts of what happened, along with the facts and figures on the deportation of ethnic Poles in Belorussia, who lived there for ten centuries, sent to the Polish People's Republic from regions annexed by the Soviet Union. He fled to East Berlin, which still had an open border with West Berlin, bribed a guard to cross, and flew with other refugees to Cologne. Why he didn't stay there, I don't know. Sorry, I'm talking a lot. I talked too much as a boy; too much for my father, anyway."

Louis had never been as homesick as he was then, he confessed. He hoped I would agree to room together, not wanting to be alone, and had thought me most likely English, noticing my shorn hair and trainers and that all trains from the English Channel arrived at Gare du Nord.

"The receptionist didn't mind us sharing," I said, "despite the creaky floor right above her desk."

"She must have men coming in all the time, being beside the railway, with Pigalle just a few hundred metres away in the ninth arrondissement. Places like these have a long history of manual workers from the northern towns, *les classes dangereuses*, cruising for Paris gentlemen."

"So we're in good company, then — a shrine to our ancestors."

"I'm surprised there are no commemoration plaques thanking us for the business, to be honest. There should be. And now look at what's happening. There's talk of tattooing us and sending us to quarantine camps."

He darted up at a creak of the hallway floor outside, warning me with hooded eyes to keep silent. Two men chatted outside our door. He crept toward the edge of the bed, wrapping his fingers around the post as if holding a grenade, and froze. His knuckles turned white, gripping the finial. The voices receded down the hall and he returned to bed, barely glancing at me before putting his arm back around my shoulder.

"Sorry, I thought they were going to knock and we'd have to get dressed."

"How did you get that scar on your skull?"

"My father liked to aim for the head."

Louis asked me about my parents. I explained they had fired me when I was thirteen, having no interest in raising me, being far too fey and rebellious, and that my relatives had no wish to take me in (not that I would have wanted to live with them), so I ran away.

"I had a passport," I said, "which my parents secured for me when I was young, so I wandered around Europe. I've lived on the street ever since. No place I've ever been is more foreign to me than the circumstances of my upbringing. Anyone could get a bed and a meal for cleaning toilets and mopping floors in youth hostels. Men supported and provided for me; some asked for sex and others didn't. But I was desperate for it when I hit puberty. As soon as my voice changed, I was horny. All day, every day."

"I slept with as many boys as possible in Verviers," he said, "then found more on day visits to Brussels, and was always back in time for my curfew."

"I was eager," I said, "but young and complicated. A walking fire alarm. As if I was catching up somehow, despite just hitting puberty. I'm convinced it was genetic, or spiritual. Since then, I haven't spoken to my family. Sometimes I attended school, staying in squats or with friends, until the catastrophe of the last few years, and the vile public reaction, forced me over an abyss. So celebratory, as if a sudden snap of frost had mercifully killed off all the flies."

The afternoon light fell on our skin, and the drawn curtains gave the walls a grey-blue tint. I propped myself up on my elbow and stroked his arm.

"I don't want to offend, but I've never seen that much cash on one person. Why are you carrying so much money? You were nervous when you saw the police and anxious when you looked outside. Are you connected to those bombings?"

Louis was silent for a long time. Then he sat up, ran his fingers through his hair, and pressed down on his head.

"I can't go back to Belgium," he said. "I'm not sure how long I can stay in France, and it's best if I leave in the morning because I'm acting on plans before I finish making them, which is why I look nervous, worried that impulse will cause me to make a mistake. For today, I'm grateful we spent time together. Please stay the night with me since I don't know when it will happen again. You're in no danger."

He reached for his bag and took something out of the pocket. I thought it was a gun or a garrotte wire, and I was about to die. My stomach tightened.

"You can see from my passport, which I didn't give the hotel clerk, that I am who I say I am."

He handed me his passport: Louis Korol, born August 12, 1960.

"I moved to Brussels at nineteen, apprenticing with a famous cordwainer who manufactured bespoke shoe forms for design houses, mostly Italian and French. Michel used to come into the shop. After being intimate with his feet for over a year, we finally went on a date. He was a teacher of mathematics, ten years older. We moved in together too quickly for his friends, who cautioned us to move slower, but I'm very domestic. When he became ill and was hospitalized last year, I thought it was bronchitis."

He sat up, extended one leg, then tucked his foot under his knee.

"We built a life, but it was an illusion. One by one, things fell apart. Michel was held in an isolation unit. Because I wasn't a relative, they refused to let me see him. With the help of a sympathetic doctor, I fought for his release. So I cared for him in our apartment, alone. Some friends refused to visit. They were afraid and abandoned us. A few were loyal and helped when they could. The infections were beyond anything I ever imagined. He was blind in one eye, had meningitis in his brain and spine, and was infected with a fungus only found in Asian rats. An experimental drug left him disfigured."

Louis gazed at the washed-out Cézanne on the wall, tilting his head.

"At first, I didn't think I could do it, but it's strange what the heart can bear. When I strangled him, it was like squeezing a balloon in the middle; the top and bottom of the neck expanded, and the skin was raw and red. That's the image that stays with me. A balloon. I washed his body and stayed with him until the evening. His throat was turning purple when I finally left. I hoped there would be spiritual relief, at least. I wanted to feel something moral. But I was wrong. What's the saying in English about silence being too loud?"

"Silence is deafening."

"There is no goodness, no evil. There is only horror at the end, pain and blood, no redemption or conclusion. No salvation. Time jumps, your world is erased, and there's nothing left but a black void."

"Louis, where is the body?"

"I called an undertaker from a phone box at the station, withdrew our money from the bank, and left the city on the first train to Ostend. It was deserted the entire week, being the middle of winter. The light was heavy, like a blanket. I walked along the deserted beach in the early mornings and evenings. The freezing, salty air cleared my head, and I ate my meals downstairs or in my room."

"What made you choose Paris?"

"I can move easily between Benelux countries: Holland, Belgium, and Luxembourg, and they say we will have open borders with Germany as soon as this summer."

He laughed and shook his head.

"But thanks to my father, I don't speak German. I had to go as far away as possible, first to France where I knew the language and no one would ask me questions, then somewhere safer. Crossing the French border is simple, but it was the first test. The train to Paris connects in Brussels. Seeing soldiers in the station made me uneasy, but I had read about the bombings. Seeing so many of them in Paris, I panicked, thinking they were checking passengers. I thought about boarding a train right away."

He took my hands and rested his forehead against mine.

"Sitting at the station today, I lived my father's life over again. Unconsciously, I had completed the circle. Back to his arrival here, before my birth, his exile ending where mine begins. I recognized you immediately. The signs we use. When you walked by, staring at me, I knew you. When I saw you, I took a chance."

I WOKE BEFORE DAWN. ON THE SINK, OUR TOOTHBRUSHes were lined up side by side and a folded square of toilet paper had been tucked underneath the brush heads. Louis slept through the night, but his body jerked and twitched. There was no sunrise; the charcoal sky just turned cement. When light coursed through the curtain's crack, and the sound of trucks and shouts of men began outside, we forced ourselves up and dressed for the day. Louis gave me his cap.

"It fits you better," he said. "Besides, I have a watchman's toque that is less noticeable."

"Where will you go?"

"To Spain or Morocco, maybe, or to an English-speaking country. I have to keep moving and can't see anyone I know for now."

We drank coffee, just the two of us, downstairs. It was thick and very sweet. I told him to write to me care of Post Restante, Great Portland Street, in London and gave him the address. After we took the stairs, I watched him walk across the parking lot and vanish around the corner in his toque, and I never heard from him again.

CHAPTER TWO

YURI KATO

I n June 1989, I lay in the long grass with my friend Yuri Kato in the Parc des Royaux, filled with mature Norway maple, red ash, and European linden trees, cradling a yellow Pyrex salad bowl covered in cling wrap. The park bordered an unassuming side street off Rue Sherbrooke in a bleak section of the Sainte-Marie neighbourhood of Montreal. The summer haze was thick and rather disagreeable, and we were in our usual collective denial about the coming endless winter. We were early for a potluck dinner at a modest, three-storey terraced walk-up, a Catholic Worker house run by our friend Johann, based on Dorothy Day's teachings of non-violence and communitarianism, providing food and accommodation for refugees and the homeless, where Yuri and I had been volunteering.

When we finally knocked, Johann greeted us with his usual Cheshire cat grin in an apron that said EL JEFE in embroidery on the front. He ushered us in, handing me a cheese grater.

"For the pasta casserole, if you can give me a hand, dear."

"Oh no. I'm afraid I've brought macaroni salad. And Yuri has potato."

"Starch, then. Don't tell my trainer, he's such a harridan. Everyone's gone out, but a few residents will join us for dessert. I made a bundt."

Johann was soft-spoken and magnanimous, with rimmed spectacles, shaggy hair, and a thick moustache. He was sexy, irreverent, and committed to radical non-violence. Being an atheist, I admired his conviction but shared none of his beliefs. He resisted cynicism and rejected calls that his ideas were naive with a throaty chortle. A mutual friend called him "the most good-natured zealot you will ever meet."

After setting the wobbly table and a few aperitifs, we dug in, and Johann turned to Yuri.

"You were overseas, weren't you? Before coming back to the city?"

"I worked briefly in Guatemala in the civil war," Yuri said. "In the far north, then in the capital."

"And you, darling? I never asked what made you come to Canada."

"I moved for love," I said, "being sure it would last forever. But it was only lust."

"The dreaded long-distance crush."

"Still, I decided to stay for a while."

Yuri passed me the plate of green beans and gestured to Johann. "How did you two meet?"

"I don't remember meeting Johann the first time," I said, "but it was in early 1986. Was it a protest? A political meeting? A pub?"

"The three P's. A trifecta of queer life," Johann said. "I don't recall the first time either. But it wasn't carnal. There was absolutely no sexual congress."

"There are many strangers with whom I have forgotten I slept," I said, "but I always remember sleeping with my friends."

"And we did not."

"I was most likely rebuffed, my pride wounded. Every rejection after my broken heart was a verdict on my character."

"And I've never slept with Yuri either," Johann said.

"And Yuri and I have never slept together," I said.

"Goodness gracious, someone call the media," Johann said. "There's been a unicorn sighting."

Yuri was now canvassing door to door for charity, spinning his wheels. I stared at Yuri as he spoke: the thick, black hair growing down his nape and brushing his ears, the mole on his smooth cheek, and the gap between his front teeth. In summer, I would watch his lithe body, the sinuous tendons in his feet, and the sharpness of his shoulder blades. Despite his introversion, he was generous with compliments and patient with unpleasantness, making him much more suitable than me to work in Johann's house, where people struggled with addiction or settlement issues, the effects of torture or political persecution, and the threat of deportation.

"Yuri's Spanish has been a godsend with new arrivals," Johann said. "Mine is useless."

"Yuri speaks Japanese, French, Spanish, and English," I said, "which, as a shamefaced monolinguist, impressed me to no end when we met."

"You're very cute together. Do you know you finish each other's sentences? Occasionally you are granted a friendship above transgression," Johann said. "Daily moods and moral failures don't need forgiving. Their insignificance is assumed."

Johann refilled our wineglasses, slid a cardboard coaster under the table leg, and opened another bottle between his thighs. Yuri swayed in his seat.

"My first lover, Alfred, was forty-six when we met," Johann said. "It was the mid-1960s at an early emancipation meeting. He was born in 1920 and became a pacifist after seeing Calder's *Mercury Fountain*, Picasso's just-completed

Guernica, and Miró's *The Reaper* at the Spanish pavilion of the International Exhibition of Art and Technology in Paris in the summer of 1937. I was already a smart-ass and political at twenty-one, so I followed Alfred around like a puppy until he agreed to sleep with me, most likely from sheer exhaustion. The long on-and-off affair only ended a few years ago. He was dead within a matter of weeks."

After saying good night, and too many bottles of wine, I held Yuri's arm as we took the porch stairs.

"I'm glad you didn't sleep with Johann," I said.

"Why?"

"I would have been jealous."

He scrunched his face and scoffed, tripping over his feet.

IN EARLY AUGUST, YURI AND I SLUMPED ON THE TOP bleacher beside an empty, gravel-covered baseball diamond, where we often came to drink and daydream. He had received his positive diagnosis the week before, but I was the one who had been bawling for days.

"I've organized an extended tour of Europe," he said. "Will you come with me?"

My eyes lit up. "But what about the doctors?"

"My specialist wants to start me on an aggressive treatment, which she warned was toxic, but I refused. I asked her only for a medical letter certifying the prognosis and a copy of my blood tests."

Yuri's T-cell count was dropping fast, and he had lost weight, which at first wasn't that noticeable on his lissom frame, but his pallor changed. His skin was dull and yellowish, and he suffered from an uncomfortable breakout of molluscum contagiosum warts over his body, which was why he had gone to the clinic.

"But we have no money."

"Actually, we do. I've sold my life insurance policy."

"To whom?"

"Who knows? It's a death benefit payout, called a viatical settlement, to some third party. Cash upfront, for half its paper value, to be paid in full to the new policyholder when I die. Investors seek returns. I guess word got out amongst ambulance chasers that this was easy money, with no risk and an almost guaranteed return. The sum isn't extravagant, but I can now pay for the entire trip. And I don't plan on dying."

WE ARRIVED IN MUNICH THE LAST DAY OF AUGUST AND stayed with Yuri's ex-lover Rainard in the Haidhausen neighbourhood, whom Yuri met as a visiting student at Ludwig Maximilian University and spent the week planning an open-ended itinerary circling Western Europe. Rainard's friend, a middle-aged man with a rash on his neck and a fast Mercedes-Benz, drove us to West Berlin, explaining there were no speed limits on the motorways in West Germany, as he would prove.

On the journey, ramparts enclosed both sides of the highway until we passed through Leipzig and slowed our speed. The high walls gave way to barbed wire and fencing, and I saw the backfield of a sports facility. Around a worn, dated running track, groups of men darted out of starting blocks and threw javelins. I remembered the rumours of doping by swimmers and track-and-field athletes from East Germany, and the sole glimpse I caught of the entire communist German Democratic Republic was of muscular athletes training in singlets and shorts. On our first night, we stayed at a modest hotel in Schöneberg and attended a free meeting arranged by the British Council across the street. Speakers from the East described escapes to West Berlin through secret tunnels, hiding under false floors in the trunks of cars, and even by tightrope. One man swam the Teltow Canal south of the city for over five hours in 1966, evading border guards, and returned multiple times, rescuing over thirty people, until he was caught and imprisoned before the West German authorities secured his release four years later. It wasn't risking escape; it was returning for others, again and again, that awed me.

Early the next morning, we walked past the glowing church tower of the Kaiser Wilhelm war memorial in dense fog, strolling through an empty Tiergarten to the new Rosa Luxemburg monument, her name spelled out in thick bronze letters at the spot where, after she was tortured and murdered, her body was thrown into the Landwehr Canal in 1919. These memorials were two rarities in West Berlin. It was an undocumented city, an apparition, cleaved in half, its axis askew. Subversive, visceral, and plundered — a perfect place for exiles. It didn't thin out into the countryside like other cities. Walk straight ahead in any direction and you hit a wall or barrier. And so its inhabitants learned to move in circles. There were emotional and historical dead ends in every district: bullet-scarred walls, piles of unexplained rubble, and streets that led nowhere. With each abandoned building, you felt the burden of history, yet it remained a tabula rasa. You were blind to its meaning. At Yuri's urging, we visited the former site near our hotel of the first Tuntenhaus, a now-renovated neoclassical apartment on Bülowstrasse, where a group of homosexual squatters created a self-directed community in 1981. Although illegal, it lasted until 1983 or 1984, even after the leader of the squatters' movement was hit by a bus and killed while protesting for housing rights later that same year. Yuri had dated a Tuntenhaus resident named Karl. The neighbourhood was typically eclectic, repurposed, an amalgam of styles and histories that created its own unique story and energy. A severe Lutheran church spire dominated a skyline of brutalist buildings and modern postwar apartments with their large loggias. The elevated art nouveau U-Bahn station with an immense glassed-in train shed and decorative exterior pylons had been decommissioned with the expansion and fortification of the Berlin Wall. By then it was a station to nowhere. A Turkish bazaar had been installed along the platform, a covered market lined with permanent kiosks: a pentimento. Former subway cars sat on the rail lines under the iron columns and glass facade. From outside it looked to be operational (except for one vintage cream-coloured streetcar parked at the end of the concourse), but it was now being used for selling stacks of sweet figs and dates, bags of candied chestnuts, dried fruit, and boxes full of almonds, hazelnuts, and pistachios. A line of kiosks beside the old tram car sold small household and commercial items, where we purchased notebooks for our journey.

As night fell, I watched Yuri walking alone along the bustling platform, with the wails of shopkeepers floating through the smoky light, like the photographs of improvised open-air markets among the ruined buildings after the war: people pawning rotting shoes, embroidered bits of tablecloth, and single discoloured spoons, only now they hawked an abundance of goods down the rails from the longest urban fortification of the twentieth century. We left the station, taking the stairs, and crossed through the underpass, stopping at an empty beer hall under the tracks.

After a drinking contest lasting two hours, which I handily won, Yuri clutched his drained stein like a lifebuoy and hung his head.

"I was just thinking of my sister, Hana."

He had mentioned his sister's disappearance to his friends but never went into detail.

"You haven't told me what happened to her."

"She vanished on the country road by our family home, walking to a neighbour's house for a sleepover only a hundred metres away. She was ten years old. It was daylight. I remember the bare tree branches against an overcast sky from the window, with a thick carpet of golden leaves turning brown along the shoulders. She carried a lunchbox full of snacks for the evening and a carrier bag with her folded grey-and-pink terry-cloth pyjamas. When she didn't arrive after an hour, the neighbour telephoned to ask if she was still coming. The Laval police organized a search party that night, which continued for a month. After three years waiting for her return, we moved."

He burped, letting out an extended breath. "The government started a scheme with the Canadian Dairy Commission. Do you remember? It publicized missing children on dairy products, hoping someone called with a clue to their whereabouts. For years, I saw the grainy black-and-white photograph of my sister on the milk I bought from the store. My mother never admitted to seeing Hana on a carton, but the original picture was banned from our house without explanation. In a panic, I once went to the supermarket and searched through the entire fridge for Hana's photo, chucking every carton until the staff kicked me out."

Yuri fumbled for his wallet and showed me the photo. "I expected my parents to be smothering after that. Curiously, they did the opposite. We became more and more estranged, and in the end they divorced."

"That's not your fault."

"Maybe when they looked at me, they were reminded of Hana, or she'd secretly been their favourite, and they held an unspoken resentment. I'd catch them out of the corner of my eye, staring at me with dread. When I came out, my parents insisted on taking me to a psychiatrist. It was a long, drawn-out drama. Eventually, I stopped hearing from them."

He ordered another round from the passing server as if he was flagging down a car.

"I'd like to go to Turkey," he said.

On the way home, in the sodium light outside the squatters' apartment building, Yuri slow-danced with a lamppost and spoke to me in tears about Karl. They lost touch over the years. Letters were returned and phone numbers were no longer in service.

"I followed the movement from university, trying to start a housing collective in Munich without success. I assume Karl is dead. Like everyone else. That feeling never left me, that all my acquaintances must be dead. Do you have the same? And tonight, I realized Hana's also dead. I know it."

FROM BERLIN, WE FLEW TO ISTANBUL, MONEY BELTS filled with cash and traveller's cheques. As soon as we arrived, I knew we had made the right decision. On a small riverside hotel balcony on the European side, the salt spray from the Bosphorus Strait brushed our faces. The room was panelled in pale wood, with twin beds covered in pink silk sheets and bath towels folded daily on top into the shape of swans. Sketches of the Hagia Sophia, Blue Mosque, Yedikule Fortress, and Topkapi Palace dotted the plastic tablecloths on the breakfast tables in the rooftop restaurant. We visited them all over the coming days. The spice bazaar was just over the road from the hotel, where we strolled directionless through halls smelling of cumin, ginger, and black pepper, past stalls laden with smoked spices, saffron, jellies wrapped in colourful paper, candied pralines, garlands of bright marigolds, and shelves of golden honeyed sweets. On Yuri's insistence, we smoked shisha many afternoons under the bridge until sunset, while fishers and shrieking seagulls vied for the

day's catch, and wandered the Fener neighbourhood's colourful streets, past Greek Orthodox seminaries and Jewish syna-
gogues, taking the ferry across a stormy channel to hop on a
rickety single-carriage tram.

With its narrow wood frame, porthole headlights, and
Jazz Age marquee, it looked just like the tram parked at the
end of the platform at Bülowstrasse station. The last stop was
Dolmabahçe Palace, which wouldn't have been out of place
in Venice. A veil of drizzle hung over the day, glazing the
city and turning its colours a shade darker. Istanbul metro's
first six stations had opened two weeks before, and heady
passengers crowded the platforms. We rode the M1 line from
Aksaray Station to the working-class district of Kocatepe,
wandering through the Bulgarian and Yugoslav migrant
tenements and industrial back streets, where old men sat
playing tabla outside cramped restaurants that smelled of
burning fruit, and boys sold raffle tickets from folding tables
on the sidewalk. Alleys were crammed with booksellers, tiny
stores boasted tools, bolts, and screws of every size, and mer-
chants hawked brass cups, platters, and kettles from under
plastic tarpaulins. Inhaling diesel and frankincense, we ended the walk at the grand mosque, one of the world's largest,
only finished a few years before. The original modernist design, by a former mayor of Ankara, was hailed as a master-
piece and meant to usher in a new age showcasing pluralism
in Islam, but furious opposition by a newly formed group of

conservative clerics stopped the plans after the foundation was laid. Instead, the mosque built nodded to the Byzantine and Iranian styles so favoured in Ottoman architecture.

Late in the evening in a fine rain, we went to find a bar near Taksim Square, appropriately called Vat 69, which I had read about in *Spartacus*, an underground gay travel guide that was normally out of date as soon as it was in print due to the itinerant nature of illegal establishments. Using a map, we walked south under the awnings from the metro station and turned left down a steep street lined with tall buildings in Çukurcuma. By a fork in the road, next to a tiny food stand with a Coca-Cola sign, we opened a nondescript steel door. An elderly man sat by another reinforced door down a red hallway. Inside, we descended into a high-ceilinged basement club decorated with black velvet paintings of running horses, tropical beaches, and moonlit waterfalls. The clientele was a mixture of Turkish drag queens with Balkan-style blouses, lace aprons, and pleated skirts, older men with bushy moustaches in dark day suits, a smattering of tourists, and a loud group of young local men in jeans and T-shirts at the bar. The music was a mix of Boney M., Turkish folk songs mixed to disco, and U.K. dance hits by T'Pau and Mel and Kim.

We drank too much. As we waited for another round, Yuri said he wanted to stay late. I was noncommittal but left him at the counter and went to our table, sulking. Watching him from a distance, I imagined him as a stranger, gaunt and pallid alone in the dim blue light, the bones on his wrist and hands lacking flesh, his jawline prominent, and his movements awkward and unsure, clinging to something the world was determined to steal. Yuri cruised a group member at the bar, his eyes staring a bit too freely. I despaired as the young man unsubtly turned his back. Yuri returned to the table.

"We can stay if you like," I said.

"I'm fine to leave."

On our way home, I yearned to reach out or say something meaningful as we walked to the station, but he kept his distance, and I felt trapped in my own desolate emotions.

Yuri seemed cheerful enough back in our room, sitting outside, watching the glow of city lights reflecting off the black water. As I fell asleep, horns and the salt air rushed in from the open sliding door. I awoke from a drunken slumber very late. He was still on the balcony, his back to me, finishing *Fodor's Turkey 1986*, discovered on a shelf by the check-in desk the day before. When he went to sleep, I climbed into Yuri's bed in the darkness. I wrapped my arm around him from behind and felt his body tense and breathing stop.

"I want you to fuck me."

Yuri froze. I stroked his shoulder. Without turning, he pushed my arm away.

"Go back to your bed."

I crawled into my bed, facing away from him. When I apologized, I heard him turn. His voice was gentle.

"Long ago," he said, "we promised to be there for each other when this terrible night ends. Well, we won't make it. I chose you to steer this ship with me, and we're alone on it now. But I don't touch your arm. I don't lean into you when I speak or put my head on your shoulder when I'm tired, all the natural things I would do otherwise. My eyes don't linger on you because I know it will spark that hope of romance, the signals I'm wary of giving, so I do nothing you could misinterpret. It exhausts me, and my body has no more energy to take care of your heart. When I share intimate details of my life, I leave out anything that would make you jealous. You are put out when I date other men, and so I've never fallen in love with anyone since we met for fear of having to choose between you, which would break my heart. But the dejection has become an addiction for you, an intemperate obsession I've prayed will cure itself and yet you give me no peace. You force your fantasy onto me. There's a scrim of your making between us I don't dare puncture. I can't leave you because I love you. You're the best friend I ever had, but the tension it causes is so debilitating I fear it's killing me faster. So help me stay alive and make this voyage or stand aside if you can't let go of your selfish feelings. Either way, once you've made your choice, we'll never speak of this again. If you can't, I'll continue on alone."

With that, I heard him turn over in bed. My shame leached into every corner of the room, smothering the darkness.

"I choose to help. I want you to live."

As I closed my eyes, his words cut into me like shards of glass: *You give me no peace.*

THE FOLLOWING MORNING, LIFE RETURNED TO NOR-mal, and Yuri was fine at breakfast.

"I want to go to Eastern Turkey," he said.

"Why?"

"Right away. We can travel by boat along the Black Sea coast. One leaves Wednesday at sunset. Will you join me?"

Over the next two days, we set out to the bank, travel agency, and Turkish Maritime Lines ticket office to book passage on a steamer from the port of Istanbul to Trabzon, near the Soviet border, a journey of almost four days.

On the evening of our voyage, we waited on an empty platform to embark, a pink sun hanging in the sky.

"What made you choose this destination?"

He shrugged and looked east across the waterfront. "It was the guidebook's shortest section."

On the voyage, I saw only mountains, all green or grey. The boat floated under a moonless night. Only the rumble of engines and the odd stray cluster of lights on the shore proved we weren't suspended in a distant galaxy. Our bunk was compact and airless, and I stared into an ashen sea so flat it absorbed any light, a sky of leaden cloud, but a coastline of the deepest viridescence. We moored one dull, cool morning on the isthmus of Sinop, by the town of Samsun, where I struck up a conversation with the ship's purser.

"Three hundred kilometres to the north lies the Sea of Rostov," he said, "and Soviet Ukraine."

"I'm afraid it means nothing more than a vague, awful image of a fifty-year-old famine from a history text in high school."

But turning southeast out of the port while Yuri slept off a new fever, nearly veering into a line of four unidentified naval vessels heading in the opposite direction, a strangeness caught my eye. As the light grew and the hour passed, the land emptied and flattened. A storm threatened from the northeast but never came, and we sailed near a series of endless runways paralleling the coast. Squat buildings resembling hangars stretched toward plains in the south, yet there were no signs of life. No towns or villages interrupted the coastline, as if time had stopped. Passing one runway by the shore, I saw a single fighter jet ready for takeoff. I watched it ascend almost vertically, bank north into a thunderous sky, and vanish. Feeling drops of biting rain on my face, I coiled up, folded my arms around my waist, and sat myself on the deck for the rest of the day.

A FALL MIST ARRIVED, THE AIR WAS CRISP, AND THE FIRST trees had turned dark orange when we disembarked in Trabzon, a strange city in every respect, more like the Black Forest in southwest Germany or the hills of Switzerland than anything we had seen in Turkey, sitting on a glassy inlet, its red gabled chalet houses surrounded by woodland mountains. As picturesque as it was, we stayed only long enough to sleep and chart an onward route south. Yuri was losing more weight and looking sallow. A private car took us past an impressive waterfall to Sumela Monastery, carved into a sheet of rock twelve hundred metres high on a pointed mountainside in the Pontic Alps. The monastery's origins were a mystery, but from the breathtaking frescoes in the cliff face, it dated to at least the fourth century and now sat abandoned, overlooking a deep valley.

We flew south to Malatya in Eastern Anatolia and hired a driver for two weeks through the small tourist office at the airport. Bahoz, our Kurdish-Iranian guide, who had lived in Turkey for much of the 1980s, had such a commanding voice that he sounded irate on the telephone. Upon meeting, we found him such an agreeable companion and put ourselves in his capable hands.

We stopped first at Mount Nemrut, deep in the Taurus Mountains, at the temple-tomb of Nemrut Dag, a series of Greek Persian megaliths that had just been declared a UNESCO Heritage Site. Near the summit, massive stone human, eagle, and lion heads dotted the limestone terraces, severed from their bodies on the cliff face above. Sandstone steles of warriors lined the western terrace, with a view of the empty ranges of Adiyaman Province. We drove through the walled Kurdish city of Diyarbakir and across chartreuse fjords, past goat shepherds, creviced canyons, and herdsmen on donkeys tending their thousands of sheep. The verdancy gave way to wide, stony hills the colour of cake batter before the mountain approach surrounding Lake Van in the far east, where we stayed overnight on the outskirts of the city at a nondescript business hotel on the water, with orange-and-brown swirls on the carpet and cherry wood wainscotting, that our guide said was the best in town.

Yuri continued his habit of tidying up and making the bed every day before the cleaner arrived, striving for order. He moved deliberately, looking very frail, tucking in the sheets, smoothing the bedspread, and collecting the used glasses, rinsing them in the bathroom sink with trembling hands. The nightly bill for a double came to four dollars. Staying in the next room were two young women from Nottingham with whom we struck up a conversation on our adjoining balconies. Sophie and Alice were bewildered and ill-prepared for their journey.

"We stopped at the travel agent and asked for 'a little beach and a little adventure.' We were given a choice — a holiday in Ibiza or Kurdish-Armenian Turkey."

"Well, there are no beaches around the lake," I said, "but you're definitely having an adventure."

They had purchased Kurdish wool caps and mittens in bright colours to ward against the bitter morning chill, and were leaving with their minder, who wore a large red button that said "Lunn Poly Holiday Host" to look for the Lake Van Monster.

"It says in the guide that it's an Armenian dragon," Sophie said, "rumoured to cause windstorms across the water that drive men overboard from hysteria, and of such ferocity they could devour the world."

"So, all in all, completely safe," Yuri said, and we all laughed.

Sophie took a shine to Bahoz, who blushed whenever she was around, and called him "mi duck" when they met. Bahoz affectionately called her *kezeba min*, a term of endearment we found out translated as "my liver." Their attraction was mutual but doomed by geography.

After they left, we sat staring at their empty balcony.

"They remind me of when we were young," Yuri said.

"We're twenty-four."

"I mean it figuratively, I suppose. To have that sense of lightness again, not reconciled to the present. I imagine this is what getting old feels like. Remember the night we met? At that pretentious dinner? The art dealer from Oslo and the dentist from Toronto were having a contest to see who was

the bigger slut. One whore got up to eighty. You were otherwise engaged in conversation, or observing the drapery, the
evening was that dull. Then they asked how many men you'd
slept with. You said, 'Oh, I don't know, ten thousand?' So
breezily, as if commenting on the weather. The looks on their
faces were priceless."

"I revised it down after the horrified silence. Maybe five
thousand."

"That's the moment I knew we'd be friends."

A heavy snowpack glinted on the peaks, the delicate frost
on the balusters had become dew, and the lake was crystal-
line. Only a tiny boat in the distance cut the glassy surface, a
sculler making the slow crossing between the mainland and
Akdamar Island, home to an ancient Armenian cathedral
nestled in a rocky grove of apricot and almond trees, like the
oarsmen rowing Charon with his souls to the afterlife in the
famous Swiss painting by Arnold Böcklin, *Isle of the Dead*.

"I'm sorry it isn't enough," he said.

I remained silent, embarrassed by his admission, but reconciled to my present. Bowing my head, I stared at my feet.

"All right."

ON THE DRIVE TO DOĞUBAYAZIT UNDER MOUNT ARARAT,
the horizon changed. The terrain emptied, the hills

became windswept, and the sun more intense. The light had drained of colour, as if a wash of white opalescence brushed the land. When we reached the valley, the streets were cloaked in a grey haze, while the mountains glowed in the last sunlight, as if day and night had merged. Iran lay to the east, and the twin peaks of the world's most fabled mountain rose from a steep, barren plateau to the northeast, covered in wide caps of snow. The Soviet Armenian earthquake claimed fifty thousand lives and Yerevan was unreachable past the heavily fortified border. Yuri was enchanted. Tourists were welcomed warmly, and conversations started over dinner in the bazaar. Bahoz argued with a nearby group, explaining that he was trying to make them understand why men like him had fled to Turkey. Early the next day, we drove south out of town across the steppes and up a winding, desolate dirt road to Ishak Pasha, a colossal seventeenth-century palace of sand-coloured towers and domes on the crest of a high rocky outcrop. We wandered alone through the many sprawling courts, quarters, and mausoleums for most of the morning, under intricate reliefs that lined the columns, arches, and halls. Yuri stared out at the deep veins of ancient riverbeds, long dry, and over the endless parched grey and purple plains beyond, saying nothing, leaning against the fortress wall of the mosque's courtyard in the wind's hiss. He lowered himself onto the ground at the arcade's balcony, pushing his legs through the carved balustrades, catching his breath.

I knew it was the silence that lured him. Yuri was far gone by the time I understood it. As his body grew weaker, his mind homed in on a landscape from which I was excluded. With every moonrise, he journeyed further away from me. Sitting on the ledge of that mountain palace, I was terrified. A vast expanse of earth blown smooth over a thousand years, stripped of surfeits, unfolded below us, so limitless that even though it was midday, I felt we were flying at the very edge of space in a velvet dusk. There was calm and yet a threat coiled just below the surface. It wouldn't wait forever.

After not moving for an hour, he stood up and walked toward me across the court, his hair convulsing in the wind.

"I'm not going back. I never planned to return, and I'll continue eastward. Will you come with me?"

The Soviet Union was impossible, which left only Syria, Iraq, or Iran. Bahoz's family was Iranian, and he urged us to choose Iran, explaining the beauty of Kurdistan and its hospitality, the Valley of the Assassins deep in the Alborz Mountains north of Tehran, and the wonders of Persepolis. But Yuri longed to see the desert. Bahoz had a cousin who had opened a small guesthouse in the Kavir Desert in eastern Iran, hoping to attract future tourists journeying along the Silk Road from Afghanistan to Europe now that the eight-year-long Iran-Iraq war was over. Bahoz assured us we would like his cousin, as he was, in his words, "a total hippie." When we asked about visas, his face brightened. The process could be completed in a day at the Iranian consulate in Erzurum, a few hours west. He had a cousin at the consulate. Bahoz, a dual citizen, could drive us as far as Tabriz, and his cousin could take us across central Iran. I said he had many cousins, which made him laugh. Bahoz suggested staying in Kars overnight on the way to Erzurum. With special permission from the municipal police, we could visit the ancient ruins of Ani, which sat right on the border with the Soviet Union, so attendance was restricted to a few daily passes, with no cameras or audiovisual equipment permitted. Stopping in the narrow gorge or gesturing at the watchtowers was forbidden. Yuri stepped forward and hugged Bahoz tightly. I turned away, concealing my unease. Bahoz took him by the waist and helped him into the car, and we returned to town to prepare for the next day's journey.

A RUINED CIVILIZATION THAT STRADDLED THE Byzantine, Persian, and Arab empires at its height in the tenth century, Ani now sat on the edge of the Iron Curtain. Architecture unseen in Europe for another two centuries. Destroyed by the Seljuks, the population slaughtered, bodies piled ten high, captured in successive centuries by everyone from the Georgians to the Mongols, ruled by Tamerlane until his death. The collapsed city walls rested against a steep abyss. Solitary skeletons of rust-coloured cathedrals and citadels, which reminded me of the memorial at Hiroshima, were scattered along a desolate plain of overgrown grass under the watchful eye of the Soviet army. Soldiers in the towers could shoot on sight should we make any disturbance. Across a mossy green river below lay the spired ruins of long-destroyed bridges, but we dared not stop to take a longer look, for as our pace slowed, the soldiers followed our moves with binoculars.

"It should be left to crumble," Yuri said. "Neglect enhances its grace."

Bahoz drove along an empty highway under the sheen of twilight, the soft hills undulating against a wide-open sky of purple crystal, and a single low glowing star in the east, crossing the border at a village called Gürbulak. Atop a bouldered hill, a pair of limp flags hung side by side on their poles. After paying the extra fee, we held out four passports like a deck of cards, two Canadian, one Japanese, and one British, and asked Bahoz's consulate contact to choose the best nationality with which to acquire visas.

Bahoz had arranged the details of our onward travels, including a twenty-hour ride from Tabriz, with a sleep stop near Isfahan, to the town of Kur in central Iran with our new driver, Awad, who drove a battered grey Paykan, the national car of Iran, spoke no English, and touched his upturned fingers to his thumb like an aggrieved Italian in the movies, saying "kebab, kebab" in baritone, indicating a meal break. It was the only time Awad spoke. But he loved singing along to traditional music on the car's cassette player.

The next day, we would rendezvous with Bahoz's cousin Murtaza and drive deep into the Kavir Desert. Murtaza bought an abandoned village from the government and was looking to buy another. We offered to pay him a large amount of cash up front for access to a guest house or private place to stay. Bahoz had alerted Murtaza to Yuri's condition ahead of time, and Murtaza sent a message welcoming us with open arms. Bahoz saw us to Tabriz; after our farewell, he was returning home to visit what was left of his family in a mountain village near Marivan in Iranian Kurdistan to the south, where fierce fighting raged for years and had decimated the male population to almost zero. Some died as civilians and some as insurgents, he explained, as Kurds had extended family in both countries. Bahoz left after the Halabja chemical attack eighteen months earlier, where mustard gas and nerve agents killed five thousand Kurds in Iraq only miles from the border.

"The most frightening moment was when I stopped being frightened," he said, touching his heart.

In Tabriz, we stayed only long enough to sleep and buy supplies. On its outskirts, the occasional burned-out relic of a truck or a blackened house with no roof caught my eye. Yuri experienced alarming new symptoms. His fever wasn't breaking as before, and he had a fungal infection on his tongue and in his throat, but he refused to consider any change to the plan, as if, through single-minded determination, he could outrun the fiend chasing him.

I worried we possessed no medication, so in the grand Tabriz bazaar, which Bahoz said had stood for a thousand years, I searched the rose-coloured labyrinths, with a note written in Farsi by Bahoz, until I found two boxes of tetracycline and ampicillin, and bought them for a hefty price, as well as a large amount of paracetamol, but could find only mouthwash and mint lozenges for Yuri's mouth. Everywhere I went, people stopped to welcome me. I enjoyed walnut sweets with a father and son whose family had run their shop for centuries. A group of shy young women asked if they could each ask me a question, as they were eager to practise English, and I ended up in a conversation about everything from Canadian trade policy (of which I knew next to nothing) to Iranian popular music. The women were studying either medicine or engineering at the university. When I showed them the boxes and explained I had a sick friend, one woman in medical school offered to help.

"It is not possible for you, a single male and a foreigner, to call me when I am alone at home, but my brother is a practising surgeon in the city, and I will provide you with his phone number."

With the women's help, I bought bootleg cassette tapes of folk singer Mohammad-Reza Shajarian and pop star Googoosh, both of whom the country revered. I received a handful of dinner invitations to family homes just by stopping at stalls and conversing for a few minutes, and passed young men with damaged eyes, on rudimentary crutches due to a missing leg, or whose arm had been amputated at the elbow. The overwhelming hospitality couldn't conceal the weariness, physical and otherwise, that showed on people's faces, slowed their movements, and contracted their posture. I returned to find that Yuri had thrown two hats, a scarf, his raincoat, swim trunks, binoculars, collected maps, underwear, and the *Fodor's* guidebook into the corner under a side table, along with a sweater.

"I won't have any use for those anymore," he said.

Scooping up the sweater and hat, I buried my frustration and pushed the pillboxes deep into my bag.

Driving on the motorway that evening, I thought of all the things we didn't have.

WE CROSSED HALF OF IRAN IN A DAY, SKIRTING CITIES, watching the barren, moonlike landscape turn into pasture, then wide savannah, with jagged, snow-capped mountain peaks hugging the northern horizon; then, after turning southeast, into sand. The next afternoon, after hours on a desolate road crossing empty scrubland, the land turned pale, and what green vegetation that had remained outside the window became straw. The ochre mountains lost the barbed edges and turned caramel, their shape softening to meringue.

Awad sung along to the cassettes I purchased and knew every line by heart. Yuri slept in the back, using his bag as a pillow. I woke him only as we approached Kur, a dusty-looking administrative town laid out in a grid pattern of one-storey flat-roofed buildings and too many pictures of the Ayatollah. Approaching Murtaza's family home near the central roundabout, we had yet to pass a single vehicle on the road. Murtaza's uncle greeted us and went to call Murtaza on the telephone. I helped Yuri inside after paying Awad, and we said a fond goodbye. First impressions weren't positive. We were served tea and biscuits in a cramped room with much back-and-forth conversation between the uncle and his wife, until they requested, through hand gestures, we join them in the small parlour, where an ancient television with a convex screen blasted a football game. The uncle stopped chattering, and we watched the gameplay in silence for an hour.

"Is this the house we offered to pay for?"

"If it is," Yuri said, "we move on. We can't stay one day in this dreary-looking place."

Suddenly, we heard the noise of an engine turning over outside and stood up to see a young man in a short-sleeved checked shirt and green safari pants fumbling through the front door.

"I am Murtaza. Sorry for being late. The drives are long in this neck of the woods."

He had an afro curling out in every direction, thick, square-framed tortoiseshell glasses, and carried a weathered light-brown briefcase, which made him look like a slightly zany salesperson. Murtaza's face and forearms were very tanned, and he had a thin, wiry frame that suited his happy-go-lucky energy. Putting down the case, he stretched out his arms and greeted us with handshakes and sturdy pats on the back, grinning and nodding the whole time. I knew immediately he was stoned.

"Once again, I ask forgiveness. Let me run through the details. My village is a ninety-minute drive away."

Yuri and I sighed with happiness.

"Your stay is arranged in two villages — one that I own and another that is abandoned, just over the dunes, depending on how much privacy you desire."

Murtaza opened his briefcase. "I apologize again. If we could settle the payment before leaving, as there is a safe box here, so I don't have to worry about carrying such large amounts of cash in the glove compartment."

The uncle's eyes widened at the stack of U.S. bills we gave Murtaza, and we packed up the car, a beaten-up silver Peugeot 504 from the early 1970s, which Murtaza explained he could still get parts for under the sanctions.

"I pray to the God of France every day," he said, as we drove off. "Wait until you see my pickup truck."

He thanked us over and over for paying up front. "The look on his face! My uncle, who has never seen bills of that size before, will never again say I am wasting my life or criticize my capital ventures."

Murtaza grinned, tapping the steering wheel, and his wild curls bounced in the scorching breeze from the open windows as Yuri chuckled in the passenger seat.

I realized it was the first time he had laughed in days. The back seat vibrated from the asphalt as we drove for over an hour northeast, deeper into the desert. Mountains with edges like ripped paper had given way to a smooth sheen of amber sand. Whipped peaks of dunes swelled in the distance to the left, which we turned toward, along a paved road only wide enough for one car. The sky was so white I couldn't see the sun. After twenty minutes, we veered right, travelling on an unpaved side road, a cloud of dust belching behind us, until a small patch of deep green appeared in the haze. We hadn't passed a car since leaving Kur. When we reached the village of Khazar, a dozen abandoned-looking domed adobe houses lining both sides of the street set in a slim belt of date palms, we saw two men waving at the curb. Murtaza bounced from the car to help Yuri out of the passenger seat. The men shook our hands. Hassan was tall, with a long ponytail and a goatee. He had an angular face with hazel eyes and spoke perfect English. Parviz was short and sinewy, the same build as Yuri had been, with a round face and dark eyes. He had closely cropped black hair, a curly Raj handlebar moustache, and a heavy gold earring in his left ear.

"Parviz speaks no English," Murtaza said.

With his moustache, Parviz appeared older than the other man, despite both being no more than thirty.

I noticed the absolute silence. No cicadas, birdsong, or wind interrupted the stillness of the air. Only our voices cut through the quietude. To my relief, Yuri was beaming. A periwinkle-blue Ford F-1000 truck, made in Brazil in the late 1970s with a high square crew cab, was parked across the street, in front of a vintage lime-green BMW with a white racing stripe along the side: a colour bomb interrupting the sand. A feeling of standing in the heart of something very foreign overwhelmed me. Nothing disturbed the fan of leaves on the palms or the flatness of the dunes that rose behind the village, reflecting the blazing light. Even the weather had forsworn that day. Murtaza had organized everything for our arrival, including water from an upgraded well, enough food for a few weeks (with a weekly trip to collect supplies), sleeping quarters in our own adobe with sheets, pillows, and thick blankets, and outdoor seating in a private, open-air central courtyard, just down the road from their house, a series of adjacent adobes with a shared kitchen and massive atrium. Electricity was available for six hours every evening and two hours every morning. Once Yuri had had a long sleep, a bath, and dinner, we sat around a fire in their enclosure below a black impenetrable sky, getting high.

"I bought the village two years ago from family members of the dead residents," Murtaza said. "They were eager to sell, which was made easier through my contacts in the government. The three of us have known each other since elementary school. You know, there are empty villages right across this desert, mostly inhabited by only a few elderly people."

"You'll soon be landed gentry," Yuri said.

"In a nutshell, I see myself as a developer of sorts. The residents of some villages died or moved to cities; in others, everyone was killed in the war."

Murtaza's father was a high-ranking member of the Revolutionary Guard and had been a leading figure in the revolution in 1979, which afforded Murtaza cover to live life on his own terms, although he hadn't had to test the limits of that protection. They were free to do as they pleased away from the watchful eyes of the Guidance Patrol — the name of the morality police — could have dance parties, meet girls, smoke hash, and drink alcohol when available on the black market, which were all forbidden, two punishable by long prison sentences or death. Murtaza and Hassan laughed at Parviz, who they explained was depressed.

"He found his first grey hair," Murtaza said, "so he shaved his head this morning. Parviz was drafted very young and survived the war, and he is learning German."

Murtaza draped his arm around Parviz and beamed. "To impress a girl."

Hassan came from a Zoroastrian family in Yazd, a religious city in the south. "It was the primary religion in Iran," he said, "before the Muslim invasions in the seventh century."

Hassan had refused to serve when drafted. He heard stories that the army used young conscripts from minority groups in human-wave suicide attacks against Iraqi positions, so he had fled to Kerman in the Lut Desert to the south of Kavir, where he hid in the mountains for two years until he came to join Murtaza.

"Most people still don't know where I am," he said.

As the fire crackled, and I watched the smoke rise in swarms then disappear in the darkness, Murtaza and Hassan listened to Yuri's stories from Guatemala, told to these men-children living out their teenage fantasies.

"I helped document events in an indigenous community after a massacre there by government mercenaries, who took the young men away one morning, locked the remaining villagers in the church, and burned them alive. Later, I shadowed workers at an organization tracking the country's disappeared. Its leader had been abducted and his body found in a ditch off the main highway. He'd been tortured. Eating and sleeping day and night beside the staff members made their kidnapping internationally risky. I stayed until the stress was too much and I started making mistakes. One day I left the house alone. I only wanted to go for a walk on my own. In truth, I failed. Sometimes the best intentions aren't enough. That's when they sent me home."

Hassan summarized what had been said, and Parviz began a low, lilting song of lament. Yuri closed his eyes, the soft orange light flickering across his drawn face and blurring his features.

IN KHAZAR, THE DAYS MELTED INTO NIGHTS, AND nights into weeks. Murtaza took us by car to the desert salt flats of Kavir, miles of bone-coloured, desolate, biblically dry tableland, and the five of us went dune-driving in the pickup truck. It became our favourite pastime, rumbling along the crests of sand, holding tight to the ceiling bars and dropping like a roller coaster into the valley below, often getting stuck, at which point everyone but Murtaza and Yuri got out to push. Parviz ventured out solo when we stopped, spending time alone in the dunes. Murtaza explained that Parviz had fallen in love with a German girl travelling overland from Kashmir through Afghanistan (which had just ended a brutal, protracted civil war, the last Soviet troops pulling out eight months before), Iran, Turkey, and on to Europe. She stayed with him in the village until the end of her visa and promised to return as soon as she could. Parviz crouched and scanned the rippled plateau, as if waiting for a letter from the heavens or watching for a tiny figure with blond hair approaching from the west.

One day, the tires became half buried in the dune and I joked we might die there.

"It would be quick," Yuri said, "if we don't bring along supplies. We can't survive more than a day or two without water. The truck would just sink into the river of sand rising around us."

Murtaza loved listening to Yuri discuss politics, so many adventures of which he could only dream, places he had never heard of, but ideas that he found comforting and familiar. And Yuri loved to hear Murtaza's stories of the desert.

"The dunes migrate over time," Murtaza said to Yuri. "Like magnets, they repel each other in the wind and grow in the opposite direction for unknown reasons. There is singing (the Peruvians call it *manchang*) as grains of sand slide along the slopes. It gets louder as the day gets longer, and a boom is heard in the evening when no wind blows at all. Sand is chaos itself. Though its grains are solid, sand moves more like liquid or gas, and they slam against each other with such force and complexity that scientists still do not have an equation to measure every outcome."

Late in the afternoon at the end of a drive, Murtaza, Yuri, and I removed our shoes and climbed to the top of the highest dune, with Murtaza and I taking turns helping Yuri up to the crest, sitting him down to watch the sunset. Murtaza sank into a spot beside him. The wind carved soft ripples into the slope. A curtain of sand spiralled up the curving spine of the dune like a dervish, and we heard Hassan and Parviz's crystal-clear voices below to the right, fiddling with something in the cargo bed. I got up and tried to walk along the razor-sharp edge, but it dissolved, my toes sinking into the sand. The surface was burning hot, but it only took my sinking foot to hit the chill that lay below, and I trembled. Losing my balance, I slipped down the windward side, falling into shadow. When I scrambled back to the top, my face emerging into the sunlight, I saw Yuri put his head on Murtaza's shoulder. I sat in silence a short distance away.

The horizon squeezed the pink sun as it descended into the cleft between two distant shaded bluffs. From that vantage point, the sky seemed vertical. Long wisps of cirrus clouds like tree branches reached up from the earth. At noon, under a film of pearl light, the dunes appeared distant, yet in the ember glow of sunset, it was as if you sat under them.

The next morning, Murtaza drove us along the road to the neighbouring village, just on the other side of a small dune, reached quicker by walking over it from town. Burjan was no longer listed on any map. In fact, Murtaza had to go to the archival office in Kur to discover its name. Burjan was a tiny crumbling hamlet of only a few stone houses in a deep valley surrounded by lush Tamarix and other cedar trees fed by an underground spring, the same one that fed their well. A few times a season, herds of wild camels came to drink there, lingering for days until, satiated, they resumed their melancholy saunter in a broken line and disappeared over the plateau. Murtaza pointed out the droppings strewn across the lane leading to the water. Inside one house were remnants of a bedroom and kitchen, with buckets standing by the entrance, a wide, shallow cooking pan dropped in the corner, and a single mattress on the dusty floor.

"No one knows about the village's inhabitants. No one remembers their names or fates, who stayed or were the last to die, or if any were buried nearby."

I found Yuri there when, febrile, he vanished from the adobe. For an hour, I feared the worst: that he had walked into the desert; then on a hunch I grabbed the truck keys and drove to Burjan. Despite searching the canopy and lanes, there was no trace of him. Finally, I saw him on the mattress inside the ruins of the stone house, breathless but with clear eyes, gazing out the window.

I recognized the look on his face, drawn to the chaos, and dropped to my knees to squeeze his hand.

"We can go right now," I said. "Bahoz will have a cousin who can take us as far as Herat. Then we can hire a car, go overland and cross at Peshawar."

Yuri's eyes fixed on a distant point on the horizon. I squeezed harder.

"No, don't leave. Then we'll head south. Over the Karakoram to Kashmir. You want to see the wildflowers, don't you? Down through the Indus Basin, following the river. Will you come with me?"

I searched the room for something to cling to; scanned my mind for a crumb to convince him to remain in his body, rooted to the ground, and not rise over the sand into the blinding heat of the day.

"Marble palaces so white they vanish in the morning fog. Jaipur, the Pink City. Promise to stay with me?"

His drawstring pants hung loose, and his T-shirt had hiked up his torso. He curled up with his back to the wall, bony pelvis and ribs protruding, turned his gaze to me, and gently placed his other hand over mine, nodding.

"First, let me wait for the camels to return," he said.

Although he was light enough to carry, Yuri insisted on walking to the truck. He had become animated. There was more strength in his movements, and his cheeks had colour. When we returned to the village, I changed his clothes, tended the fire, and filled the pots with well water. Murtaza and I walked up to the top of the next dune to watch the sun fade, and he asked me if Yuri and I were special friends.

"No," I said, barely able to speak the words. "Only best friends. But I secretly love him."

He asked us to stay in Khazar a while longer before we moved on, and I promised to remain there until the end of our visa.

On our drives, I got out and often strolled barefoot far across the sand until the muscles in my feet ached. One day, after Yuri had a surprising episode, clawing at his skin so much he bled and screamed that devils were dancing there, I fell to my knees in the wind and never rose. Murtaza came to fetch me and brought me back to the truck. Parviz stared into the low sun nearby.

"Parviz spent the last seven years as a soldier," Murtaza said. "After pressure from his family, he answered the call to martyrdom as a teenager. He has seen terrible things. All he wants in life is love. But our culture has no room for him. His heart has grown too big for this small-minded country. And so I fear Parviz will die before he finds it, or worse, will settle for less. He is not stupid. He knows his lover sits in a café in Munich and is forgetting him. It is not her fault. She lives in a world of possibilities, and is being pulled from different sides, her attention torn, which will cause her to drift and lose focus. Soon it will be a distraction. She will stop writing him and move on, which she will rationalize as nothing but a fond memory, her time here with Parviz. She may write about it with affection in a diary or explain it to friends as a gap-year adventure, a romance described to strangers at dinner parties. Parviz will remain here in this desert, like you, dying of a broken heart, but your love must count for something. We have been at war most of our adult lives, and for nothing. It swept in like a storm for eight long years, then lifted. The borders did not move, not one square metre of land was gained by force. All that happened was everyone died. I admire Yuri because he speaks to me of the eternal nature of war, yet that does not stop him. War is not made of rock or stone; it is not metal or mineral. War is sand. It shifts, but it does not vanish. One day a new hill appears, altering the landscape, creating shadow, then suddenly the hill, having changed shape, reappears elsewhere."

I looked down at the soiled, deeply cracked skin on my heels like dry canyon riverbeds, then out at the desert, an unending sheen of gold.

CHAPTER THREE

RUDOLPH DEKKER

There are people who metabolize pain in a certain way. Because of a weariness of living or bitter nostalgia for lost youth, they become more conservative as they age. My friend Gloria wasn't one of those people. She threaded many social and political ideas together in one conversation, knitting disparate topics into a grand daily manifesto, as if there wasn't enough time left for her to carry each out individually, often speaking out of turn, and with an unexpected tenderness. At our first lunch in 2002, in a small Bengali restaurant in Old Delhi, Gloria barely ate, sitting across from me in a jade embroidered blouse, her shoulder-length grey hair neatly combed and pinned to the side. As soon as she picked up her fried pakora or kathi roll, she would drop it again to emphasize a point with both hands. She explained her history: moving to India on a renewable ten-year visa to study Buddhism after spending most of her life in San Francisco, working as a nurse through the 1970s and 1980s after coming out; her abiding love of Buddhism despite the sexism she experienced and early clashes with her Dzogchen master; her exploration of liberation theology in the early 1980s; her disgust at decades of botched American policy toward Pakistan and India. Gloria refused to live in the United States anymore under George W. Bush.

"We've reached the absolute nadir with this president," she said. "Stooping any lower is unimaginable."

Gloria had turned her back on formal Buddhist practice, but still lived by its tenets, and pushed for radical change with a group of nuns she remained close to at the Geden Choeling nunnery in Himachal Pradesh.

"My god," she said, "men and their delusions. If the lama knew what those gals were up to in the monastery."

WE ARRIVED IN THE CITY OF DHARAMSHALA IN THE Western Himalayas on a fine afternoon in the early spring of 2003. The snows had receded from the hill towns around the

Upper Kangra Valley but lay thick as whipped cream on the peaks of the Dhauladhar mountains.

"Don't be fooled," Gloria said. "In the summer, the edges of those pink mountains are flint-sharp, after the heat of the monsoon melts the snow. It stays just as a sprinkling of powdered sugar until the autumn storms come again."

Spring in the valley lasted only a month. March was still off-season in McLeod Ganj, a touristy suburb high on the mountainside, and the seat of the Tibetan government in exile, up a steep, narrow road lined with Himalayan oak and, for those few weeks before the tourist crowds descended, covered with rhododendrons.

On Gloria's recommendation, we reserved rooms up the hill from town at the Chocolate Log, a dessert café with a series of campy cottages in the back that resembled a yule log cut into sections, each section its own cabin, down to the bark-like exterior cladding. I was happy to stay for the novelty factor and the magnificent vistas over the deep green valley, with a near vertical drop to the Souli Khad River. The pension was far from the commotion of the strip, full of souvenir stalls, internet bars, and ramshackle restaurants. From a distance, the rugged, terraced construction of McLeod Ganj reminded me of Corniglia and Riomaggiore in the Cinque Terre, with their pink, lemon-yellow, and aqua-blue houses growing out of the verdant hills. On the morning of our arrival, the temperature had dipped, so a fine snow dusted the edges of the rusting steel roofs. A leaden fog descended over the winding asphalt, and with the high elevation, the air felt thin and heavy in tandem. The sun emerged as a pale disc against the pearl-grey sky; then the light gained strength and by late afternoon had burned off enough haze for a heat mist to drift off the cliffs below my room. Gloria was excited to meet her friends at a hotel bar on the main street, and I wanted to explore more of the town. The lanes were filled with locals in winter sweaters and wool slacks, with monks of all ages in red and amber robes. A group of eight people, nationals and foreigners, were deep in discussion at a corner table when we arrived.

Rudolph Dekker shook my hand and introduced himself with a strong Dutch accent. The atmosphere in the bar, which fit a few dozen, was cozy and inviting. The walls were painted dark green with mint crown mouldings, and the room smelled of wood smoke. When a patron entered or exited, a blast of icy wind from the open door refreshed the air. Flute songs played in the background. Rudolph sat at the far end of the table, tall and conspicuous; a fit, distinguished-looking man in his sixties, lean and clean shaven, with shorn silver hair, full lips, a square jaw, and bright blue eyes. He wore a navy crew-neck sweater and smiled often, his large teeth suiting the breadth of his face. From time to time we exchanged silent glances and flirting grins as the conversation drifted from the war footing between India and Pakistan since Kashmiri separatists had occupied the Indian Parliament, to the new Euro and what to do with leftover liras and guilders, the murder of Daniel Pearl, the Godhra train attack which ended with three days of sectarian rioting in Ahmedabad, where a working-class neighbourhood was set ablaze, the closing ceremonies of the Salt Lake City Olympics, South Asian jazz, and the treachery of Tony Blair. Rudolph listened, rarely speaking.

When people started checking the time, departing with waves and promises to meet again, I sat together with Gloria and Rudolph. He lived in Amsterdam-Noord, he explained, but commuted to The Hague where he worked as a solicitor with the European Union, was staying for a month at the monastery, and was divorced.

"Rudolph's a Buddhist monk," Gloria said, surprising me. "He moves in high circles, higher than mine, anyway, and can teach you anything you want to know. He's a freer thinker than most of his brethren, but he's no agitator, certainly no communist, and I'll be happy to correct any distortions."

Rudolph tilted his head back, laughing. "I wonder if you're free tomorrow for a chat," he said.

"Definitely," I said.

"Wonderful. Then I will drop by in the morning after meditation."

It was twilight and much colder when we left the bar. The three of us strolled down the main street until we reached the

Temple Road intersection. Rudolph was shy, as a boy would be around strangers. It had been one of those languorous afternoons that stretched into the evening, and we walked slowly, reluctant to leave each other's company. Rudolph and I shook hands, longer and softer than the first time. I complimented him on his silver-and-blue Breguet watch, thinking it droll that a Buddhist master would wear such an expensive timepiece. He blushed and turned away with a diplomatic smile, walking down the hill through a nocturnal fog, hands deep in his pockets, in the direction of the Tsechokling temple complex and the Namgyal Monastery. Gloria grinned and raised her eyebrows, taking my arm.

"His civilian drag is very convincing," she said.

We ascended Jogiwara Road at a brisker pace to ward off the sudden shivers, past low-storey buildings painted yellow and red, their glass-paned upper rooms washed in golden light, smothered by tentacles of green LED glow-tubing, strings of spinning purple neon lotuses, and strands of orange Chinese lanterns hanging over the bustle.

THE ONLY SOUND ON THE TERRACE THE NEXT MORNING was birdsong. Rudolph knocked earlier than expected. Not to be caught off-guard, I was up and dressed. I made us black tea and bought fresh breakfast cakes from the café, for which he thanked me. The pastries smelled of crushed cardamom and ginger molasses. We sat in the garden overlooking a valley heavy with mist, him on an outdoor chaise and myself on a club chair beside him. Gloria came out of her cabin two doors down, stopping and waving. I waved her over, but she just smiled and blew a kiss, clasping her hands behind her back and returning to her room. His day started well before dawn here, he explained, biting into a farmhouse gâteau with cream and licking the excess from his fingers.

"How is someone a lawyer and Buddhist monk at the same time?"

"One came before the other," he said. "My interest in law began when I was in my twenties, and I went back to school to study it. I was lucky, for once, and started a successful immigration and refugee practice. Through my work I met Tibetans in exile, many of whom came to Amsterdam in the 1970s, although my life as a novitiate occurred later, when I returned to Holland after living in Los Angeles in the 1980s. My daughter was ill. She experienced a series of breakdowns in adolescence, and was eventually diagnosed with paranoid schizophrenia, as they called it in those days. Her condition deteriorated and she had to be institutionalized. The strain was often unbearable for me, and I looked for an escape. My introduction to Buddhism was at first more political than spiritual. I was assigned a young man's case and became very fond of him and tried to provide for his security. His parents disappeared in Tibet, and he had fled the occupation with his brother, who was by then dead. I desperately needed some peace in my head but was never a religious person. Like most people, I found organized religion disagreeable. Meditation and tantric study were the only things that eased my pain. When I felt doubt, my commitment doubled. I blossomed in the system, and it is a system. I eventually landed here, at the monastery, in advanced study to become a monk, and I return often. But time catches up to you."

"We're all running from something," I said.

"It's funny. For most of my life, I would have said I'm running from unrest."

Rudolph stared into the haze, his brow furrowed.

"Now it often seems I'm running toward it. Monastic study gave me great joy, but the closer I came to *ārya*, or the path of seeing, and the longer I devoted myself to the attainment of the six perfections, what we call *pāramitās*, the harder it has become to focus."

With a mischievous grin, he reached for the tea and took a square of ginger cake.

"I understand little about Buddhism," I said, "and fear I'll disappoint you, as I'm spiritually paralyzed and not religious at all, and I know what happens at death — nothing."

"Neither are many monks. Buddhism is a philosophy more than a religion. In that way, it's individualistic and not monotheistic, especially here. Yet it's a riddle wrapped in a mystery (or whatever Churchill said about Russia), more the longer one stays. Tibetan Buddhism places more emphasis on textual study than other branches, but within it, and indeed within the walls of this single monastery alone, there is an incredible diversity of interpretation and argument, pleasant though it may seem. It's flexible yet rigid, undeniably compassionate yet exclusionary, as our friend Gloria no doubt explained to you, collective yet hierarchical, open to outsiders yet very secretive. Now it must engage in politics. Like any journey, the road is messy, even dangerous for the uninitiated, marked by opposite extremes. Red is red or red may be blue, depending on which master you ask. Your lack of belief isn't far off from our own. Buddhism says that in the centre of the spirit, there is nothing. That emptiness is what every monk seeks to attain. In that respect, we share something in common."

"I prefer my nothing to yours. There's too much pain to do it again."

Rudolph patted my arm.

"Perhaps you and I seek the same thing," he said. "It's the avenues we have taken that diverge. But then, the next lama may tell you differently. That's the beauty of the system. I said it sounded like one big riddle."

He laughed, taking his hand away and opening his arms to the mountains. The mist had cleared, save for a white net that crept along the lower valley, then disappeared into the trees.

"Why the late rupture in your practice?"

"I could tell you facts and figures," he said, "but it wouldn't help. Can I propose a hike tomorrow? We can trek in the forest, walk amongst old growth, and visit a lesser-known nearby landmark."

After Rudolph left, and a late lunch at the hotel, I wandered around the back streets to a bluff at the top of which stood a half-finished apartment building, a steel garden of rebar rods sticking out of its cement roof. The sky was white-blue, blanching the colour from the mountain range beyond the valley, and the sun pounded on my face. The street stopped at the headland, replaced by a concrete pathway, turning into a dirt track that wound through the forest that ended at a tiny shrine visible at the edge of a promontory. I took the footpath, walking past clusters of pumpkin-coloured wildflowers and cedar trees of significant height, branchless on their lower trunks until drooping foliage cantilevered out near the crowns like an odd species of mountain palm or bonsai. I wondered if their branches had been shaved off below for some practical reason or if the trees grew this way, but it gave the woods a quixotic feeling. Stone markers, painted lemon and lime, were placed equidistant along the path like a trail of candies. Beyond that, there were no signs of habitation, save for one redbrick house draped in prayer flags fifty metres below with a flat cement roof, on which stood a shaggy, long-eared goat minding its own business. After walking for thirty minutes in the thin air, I arrived at a weather-beaten Hindu shrine with a terraced roof topped with a gold trident. The interior was rose coloured, and heavy green tailings from the iron bars stained the sides of the exterior. On a platform inside sat a steel pot, a series of small brass bells, a slab of stone with lettering, two dolls in miniature red cloaks, and a large painting of Shiva with the trident spear. Its solitude threw me off balance. At the headland, I heard a low drone in the still air. I imagined it gaining in intensity as one ascended higher into the ever-thinning atmosphere, as I had read somewhere that the universe emits a sound equivalent to B flat. To the south, a brood of heavy, darkened clouds scoped the terrain, ready to jettison their burden. I looked behind me at the houses balanced precariously on top of one another. A radio tower I hadn't seen before stood on the summit to the west. Far below, a dozen red and green tents hugged the river's edge, invisible from any other angle. With no birds singing, I heard the rushing water. A tide of shadow swept across the valley, revealing deep crevices gouged out of the mountains, the burnished light texturing the land again after the blinding glare of the early afternoon.

AN EARLY RAIN HAD CLEARED WHEN RUDOLPH PICKED me up the next morning. The sun broke through the clouds, but the air was still damp. We walked north then west on a paved road following the signs for the hamlet of Forsyth Ganj, visible at the curve ahead, stopping at the old cathedral of St. John in the Wilderness, an unlikely charcoal brick, neo-Gothic Protestant church built deep in the forest, amongst the same ornamental trees I saw the day prior on my walk to the shrine.

"Those are Deodar cedars," Rudolph said, "native to the Himalayas, divine to Hindus, and very aromatic. The foliage turns blue in sharp light. With the cathedral behind, it looks like the setting for a seventeenth-century Charles Perrault fairy tale."

To the side of the gloomy church stood an imposing, pointed-arched stone crypt with an ostentatious spire well over fifteen feet tall, topped with a brash Norman cross. I bent over to read the grave's memorial plaque. An inscription in slab serif said HE BEING DEAD YET SPEAKETH.

"Pray that's not true," I said.

"If I remember my Sunday school in Holland, the quote is from the story of Cain and Abel."

"Never one for restraint, an evangelist. Some people just never stop talking."

Up a rocky footpath on the crest of a moss-covered hill, surrounded by gravestones and soft pine, stood a white hexagonal pagoda. Rudolph led me up the path, past a bony brown ox tied to a stake in the ground, eyeing us with suspicion. Rudolph vanished behind the building. I followed him to a single marble marker with a delicate Tibetan script buried in the grass.

"It was here on this hill," he said, "where they cremated Thupten Ngodup. He set himself on fire in Delhi five years ago at a Tibetan Youth Congress hunger strike after a police raid. Chinese military personnel were visiting the capital that day. They hauled the rest of the protesters away, but he slipped past and doused himself with gasoline in a public toilet. He was a respected member of the Tibetan Special Forces, later in a guerrilla unit. After being discharged, he worked as a cook at Tsechokling, and the monastery gave him a plot of land to build a house, which was where I met him."

At that, we turned toward Naddi at the fork in the road onto a well-kept hiking trail with signs leading up the hill to Dal Lake. Before we started our ascent, Rudolph turned to me. "If I may, what brought you to India?"

"My partner, Henry, died of cardiac arrest," I said. "I left as soon as we cremated him. He was standing on a train commuting into the city, then collapsed and died instantly. For a decade, he'd tolerated debilitating trial drugs. Then years of combination therapies in the late 1990s destroyed his heart."

He went to speak, then paused and stared at the ground.
I brushed his arm.

"I was relieved for the quick death."

We walked in silence up the hill. There was an in-toeing
to Rudolph's gait, especially visible on his left side as he
skipped past the knotted roots jutting out of the earth and
snaking across our path as we reached the top.

"I love playing truant after meditation," he said, "to
stretch and work the joints after sitting in place, while other
monks stay inside to study."

"What's your position in the monastery's hierarchy?
Gloria said you were high amongst the noblemen."

"Rank and file, I'm afraid, just a novitiate. She gives me
points I don't deserve."

"For sticking it out?"

"In a manner of speaking, yes, I suppose."

"Is your stock rising or falling?"

"I will not go any further and have reached my limit. I see
myself moving to a quiet path of contemplation on my own
terms. So I would say coasting."

"Are you well liked by your peers? I assume you're not
out to them."

"Out? It's all forbidden, women or men, so the exercise
would be pointless. Releasing desire and sensual thoughts is
essential for any student on the path."

"I don't like the idea of a sensual thought police," I said.

"It gets harder the higher one goes, I admit. Amongst fellow monks, I have a reputation as a reprobate, although some appreciate my honesty. Like the black sheep in a family, as you say. Indulged, perhaps pitied. I don't say that casually; we care for each other very much. There are many others, perhaps most others, who are higher along on the path. In any system, there are open minds and closed minds, and order-keeping mandarins. I'm surely seen as having, through rigid study, reached the highest state of being possible in this life. My mentors are like spectators on their feet for the lame runner ending a race in last place. At least, that has been my impression. I suggested recently that I'm falling short, being apprehensive as soon as I took my vows, but was assured uncertainty was natural. Nevertheless, my emotions are rising to the surface more often and I've been at a crossroads for some time."

Pivoting to the right, we found ourselves at a rocky outcrop under silken clouds with a magnificent view of the lower valleys to the southern horizon. A spare, sloping woodland spread out in front of us, filled with dozens of lines of prayer flags with three stupas at the centre. Rudolph guided me to a point on the summit's far side with a steep drop into a cloud forest. I climbed onto the rock and gestured to him. He hesitated, stretching his neck and turning up his chin to see over the edge, then joined me.

"Are you in contact with your ex-wife?"

"There's friendship," he said, "even if there's no longer love. She has a partner and is happy. A tenderness remains, and we care for our daughter together and always will. We wed young, after my release from prison."

"Prison?"

"I was arrested for sexual degeneracy the first time. The law was repealed by 1971, but it was 1962."

"The first time?"

"At my first trial, I was made an example of and convicted in court with my parents present. They lived in a tiny village. My name was published in the national newspaper, which humiliated my mother. I followed a good-looking young man into a park who was undercover police. Although I understood it was forbidden, I didn't realize it was illegal. I was stripped violently at the station, thrown into a cell in the basement until my parents paid the bail, and eventually given ten years of probation."

"There was a second trial?"

"Three years later, in 1965, I was charged with indecency. As a repeat sexual offender, I was given three months in a penitentiary. I was arrested for standing longer than five minutes at a public toilet. By then, I was looking out for a type, but the officer who arrested me was middle-aged and unremarkable. When I was released, I was quite broken." He patted his left leg. "It's where I got my limp. No room for emotions or hope in such a place. That's when I went back to school to study law. I went to my parole appointments between classes. With my record, many areas of legal practice were off-limits. It took twenty years to overcome the fear of being charged again. You hold your breath every day. In the sixties, I had to convince people the condition I was convicted of was temporary. I became emotionally unavailable in my marriage as the years passed, and my wife had guessed by then that the condition was permanent. It was a relief when I spoke to her truthfully, though I couldn't tell her everything; she knows only as much as I can describe. How do you draw the outline of fog?"

Rudolph and I sat together on the flat rock in silence until he reached for my hand. I touched his thigh and kissed his shoulder.

"Doing this outside during the day was unthinkable for me a few years ago," he said.

"If you don't define yourself, others will keep doing it for you. Are you sure that's what you want?"

"I'm not sure of much anymore, but this affection is enough sustenance for me to live on for a while."

A single wide-tailed white hawk, its wings streaked with chocolate brown stripes, hovered below us, gliding against the wind. With our fingers intertwined, I stroked his thumb with my own.

AT DINNER THAT NIGHT WITH GLORIA IN AN EMPTY RES-
taurant below our hotel, which we heard stocked a few
bottles of wine, I brought up Rudolph and our hike that
morning. She was thrilled that we had hit it off so well. I
filled our wine glasses.

"Did you know Rudolph in California when he lived in
Los Angeles?"

Gloria raised her eyebrows and tucked in her chin.

"You wasted no time getting to know each other if you
know about Los Angeles."

"There's such a gaping space, such a lack of elders in my
life, that I was eager to discover more about him. I know
nothing except he lived there in the 1980s, but then I wondered whether your paths had crossed."

"Crossed paths we did. That's where we met, in San
Francisco. Rudy had driven his boyfriend, Paul, up from
Los Angeles. By then I worked at Ward 86, the first out-
patient clinic of its kind, which opened the year before at
San Francisco General, after requesting a transfer from the
University of California Medical Center. I'll never forget
the night, a year earlier, our first patient case at UCMC
was admitted to the infectious disease unit, a young man
in strict isolation, too sick to leave his bed, who received
no visitors. Apparently, someone had tried to contact the
patient's brother, but he never responded. The Bay area had
a massive storm surge that day. The Golden Gate Bridge

was closed because of heavy gusts, large swells pummelled the coast, and I was late arriving for work. While I dried my hair, I listened to the anxious conversation. There were four stations on a floor. The man's condition was quite notorious. The nurses in his unit cursed their bad luck, while other nurses in the hospital offered their condolences. One unit even sent them a sympathy card. They taped it to the wall behind the desk. The lead nurse on his ward was named Jamie. I've never forgotten her name. I passed his room from the elevator on the way to my station. A covered tray of food was always outside his door. One night, the tray was blocking the door. I picked it up and removed the cover. The ice cream had melted, the rice had crusted, and the gravy had formed a skin. I found out later that the orderly left the meal outside three times a day, refusing to enter, and retrieved it untouched. The young man in that room lasted a week. People deteriorated fast in those days, but contrary to what was on his file, he died of starvation. Patients were forced to change their own sheets. Some nurses refused to administer IVs, but it wasn't limited to one hospital. I requested a transfer to Ward 86. Believe me, there was no line to get that job."

The server placed a space heater beside our chairs on the floor. The temperature had dropped as it turned dark.

"You've never told me about those days," I said, "and their effect on you."

"It was a game of roulette, wasn't it? A few doctors were saints, but most were charlatans who targeted closeted men. Quacks lined their bank accounts and left a trail of mutilated bodies behind. Highly respected physicians were calling for a moratorium on care. No surgery. No admission to intensive care. Let me tell you, they speak now of the fear, and there was fear and plenty of it, but sometimes it wasn't fear. It was hatred. I saw it, and it was intentional. But I can't sit here and say I'm not guilty. By the summer of 1985, a group of us were smuggling unapproved drugs into the city for the most desperate. We had some success with AZT. A few lived months or even a year longer, but the rest were so toxic that we killed most people."

There were five drugs she tried to get her hands on in those years: d4T, AZT, ddI, ddC, and clarithromycin. The last was easy to stockpile as it was sold in Europe for tuberculosis. The others were smuggled in from Tijuana. The wars in Central America complicated supply lines, but they had a network in Brazil.

"But you didn't know how much to give," I said. "The government withheld data. It was criminal."

"All true," she said, "but those decisions still drag on my conscience. I'll never be rid of it, but I've learned to accept it. Dealers would sell you anything — dextran sulphate, AL-721, Compound Q derived from toxins in a Chinese cucumber. They started making huge profits, which was appalling. But when someone begs you, how do you turn away?"

The air smelled of burning dust from the heater by our feet. When a couple entered and sat in the opposite corner, the server stifled a yawn. Gloria poured us another glass of wine, which tasted tannic and cloying. It was earlier, in 1984, and before any of that, she explained to me, when Gloria met Rudy and Paul. She had taken to Paul at once. Even with the physical decline, he was so gregarious. Rudy sat in silence. They had been dating for less than a year. Rudy was on a work visa and they moved in together. Everyone was fit as a fiddle, then Paul got pneumonia.

"Paul's best friends were a couple in their early forties he'd known for over twenty years who had toddlers," she said. "They bought houses near each other in the same neighbourhood in Pasadena. I can't recall the wife's name, but the husband's name was Julius. They called Paul one day to say their doctor warned them not to have any contact, and would he please not come over anymore? They wouldn't hesitate to do the same if the tables were turned. This was about family. Around that time, Paul contracted a parasitic infection only found in deer. I recognized the signs of shock in Rudy right away. Of course I did what I could, passed along the latest research, and when that ran dry, I referred them to the Hemlock Society, which was what we did in those days, so they could end it themselves. Rudy and Paul had terrible problems finding care. Everything fell to Rudy for over a year. Once, Paul was thrown out of the hospital onto the street. Rudy fell to his knees on the curb under the Emergency sign, pleading to be readmitted."

Gloria pulled on a stray thread in her sweater.

"When he died, I drove down right away, and we spread Paul's ashes on Sunday evening. Rudy couldn't believe how white they were, but I explained emaciated bodies made paler ashes because the temperature remained high inside the oven. He didn't know Paul's disposition. It was hardly pillow talk, and there was no family in the picture, thankfully, so it was the park or the beach. If anyone discovered we spread them in a public park, there'd be pandemonium. So we drove to the beach. Rudy lost his job because he had stopped going to the office to care for Paul. The bank took the house. He returned to Holland, and we're still friends. He stopped talking about the past. When there are no words to describe something, it's easier to stay silent. He introduced me to Buddhism when we were both struggling. That's run its course for me, not without leaving a void. Women seeking to practise as equals with male monks are shunned. We're barred from debates, confined to cooking for the men or cleaning the monasteries, and forbidden from physical activities or leading prayers."

"He spins in that same solar system," I said.

She sighed. "Still, for Rudy, it was the core of his identity until recently, the only constant in his life. It brought him a measure of peace and, I assume, filled his days with a certain joy, but at a heavy price. Rudy's a respected monk, selfless and well admired, even revered in some circles, but suffers from terrible doubt. He may sing my praises for the compassion I showed them, but it's his kindness toward me over this long life that's unequalled. Anyone with decency can show compassion in a crisis. Rudy taught me a path to forgiveness, and because of him I've learned to forgive myself, which was far more complicated."

Gloria and I strolled arm in arm back to the guest house. The street was quiet, the windows and doors shuttered to the near-freezing air with just the faintest sound of a harmonium leaking from a second floor, and the air smelled of burning coal.

I SAW HIM IMMEDIATELY THROUGH THE CROWD. THE early April afternoon was bracing, the light already lengthening by midday. Rudolph had aged in the five years since we had met but had the same wide smile. Fine seventeenth-century turreted townhouses lined the serene canals of the Centrum District's Grachtengordel neighbourhood near Westerkerk Church, and single-speed bicycles fringed the herringbone-brick roads.

We sat in the window of a bright, modern café on Berenstraat and I inhaled the aroma of freshly ground coffee and scalded milk. On the table were glazed salt and pepper shakers in the shape of tiny wooden shoes. The skin on Rudolph's neck had softened, the fine lines had deepened, and his left hand trembled as he held the menu. He carried a smart-looking leather weekender bag, as he was going to Belgium by train that evening.

"Welcome to Amsterdam," he said. "Have you been before?"

"I was here in 1985," I said, "on my way to West Germany, where the parents of my first lover lived. He was forced, under duress, to leave London and move home to die because he had no health insurance in the U.K. He died a year before the disease was even discovered. It was a complete mystery. No one could explain his terrible lesions, which left him maimed. We were sleeping rough and often attacked and ended up hiding in a cemetery catacomb in Brompton. I felt something stalking us, phantoms I saw out of the corner of my eye, reflected in windows or moving in the shadows. Thinking I was going mad, I eventually went to a psychiatric hospital just to talk to someone, where I was invited in, assessed as delusional, given large amounts of lithium and phenothiazine, and sectioned against my will. I was sixteen. Soon after the first cases were reported, everyone I knew fell ill. But I was so far gone by then, paranoid and pumped up on pharmaceuticals. When I tried to kill myself in the unit, my term was extended indefinitely."

I saw him look down, scanning my wrists in vain for scars. "It was the first journey after my incarceration," I said, "and I arrived here from Paris as a nineteen-year-old. Coming here to meet you, I was remembering my arrival, turning into a bitter headwind leaving Centraal Station, accepting two slips of paper, one from a young man standing by the main doors for a hostel called the Last Watering Hole, and another from a glassy-eyed woman with a Leeds accent, about the same age as me, for a welcome meeting of the Children of God. There were twin outbreaks in Europe for travellers in those years — scabies and cults. She stopped me to ask in a hollowed-out monotone whether I was alone. From her dilated pupils, it was easy to see she was drugged. Stations across Europe were crawling with cult members from the Order of the Solar Temple, Moonies, Angel's Landing, Family, and Synanon, which won for the best name in a very competitive field."

"Many young people disappeared without a trace."

"Knowing to stay clear, I chucked her paper into the bin and headed toward the hostel, a raucous punk bar a half-dozen streets away with dorm rooms upstairs that smelled of stale sweat. The headliner advertised on the roster that night was the Filthy Urinals, so it was my kind of place. I tied my backpack around me on the upper bunk and fell asleep but was awoken in the early hours by the grunts of a young redhead on the lower bunk opposite mine, injecting heroin. I'd never seen someone shooting up before, but had a Pavlovian response to needles by then, and suddenly felt very much the ingenue, so I tried to look unruffled and stay calm, but when he approached and offered me the same needle, with serious generosity, I darted up, using my pack as a shield, which was still attached to my torso, and shooed him away. After tossing and turning through the night, eyeing the surrounding bunks, I returned to the train station. The zombie girl had disappeared. A few nights of distressing itching later, I discovered a health clinic for street youth, was diagnosed with scabies and provided a voucher for the pharmacy next door to buy Lindane, which smelled like petrol, and slathered it over my body and poured it into a laundromat machine with my clothing and sleeping bag. But it was nearly impossible to break the cycle, unless you kept it on all the time. Lindane was a neurotoxin and insecticide, developed in the 1940s by a Dutch chemist named van der Linden, who died in the year of my birth."

"My, you've done your research."

"I had little choice. For years, I used Lindane. Eventually, it was banned for causing lymphomas and cancers of the lip, testicles, and prostate, and it was why I no longer had both my balls by the 1990s. Why are you travelling to Belgium?"

"I'm going to Brussels for a few days to finalize a consulting contract at the European Commission, where I will advise on settlement policy, and to meet with the new team in charge of my daughter's care."

"How is your daughter?"

Rudolph rubbed his forehead; a web of gnarly blue veins wound along his hand and wrist.

"Since our last meeting, she continued to suffer episodes of anorexia and psychosis, which doctors diagnosed as treatment resistant. She spent six months in a supportive housing program outside the city of Purmerend, easily reachable from where I lived, with a view from the apartment window of the Waterland pastures. Bulrushes bordered a narrow canal, and cows, sheep, and horses roamed there, like the farmland of my youth. For hours, I sat with her on the small terrace, telling stories of working on the family farm after school with my grandparents. Flocks of geese flew overhead. Farmers sprayed their fields, yellow clouds rising behind them, and dogs ran alongside their owner's tractors. Describing my childhood was one way of helping her manage her illness, but her relapses became more frequent and violent. One day recently, the staff discovered her in the kitchen at midnight with a lighter in her pocket dismantling the gas stove, claiming the facility was in danger from spirits in the pipes that led in from the nearby street. In their report to the regional council, the team claimed she had nearly burned down the building and the patients in it and recommended reinstitu-tionalization. With her agreement, she was transferred to a large hospital in Groningen three hours away. A signifi-cant increase in barbiturates, antipsychotic medication, and behavioural therapies proved ineffective, and she requested psychosurgical treatment in Belgium. She will undergo a capsulotomy, where a lesion is created on the frontal lobe using a gamma knife to detach and destroy a small piece of her brain. Despite my horror and strong objections, I was convinced to proceed with the surgery after distressing meetings and coercion from both her and the doctors. My ex-wife died a few years ago, and the strain of carrying the responsibility of my daughter alone has been a heavier bu-rden than I anticipated. It comes with the usual feelings of shame. Was her illness caused by some genetic flaw I carried and passed on to her, by social trauma we could have pre-vented, or (and this may be the worst to consider) by random and intangible misfortune? Indeed, it was my monastic stud-ies that saved me from taking my life. The Tibetan centre here remains my spiritual home, and I attended a monas-tery in Groningen when my daughter was transferred, but I no longer teach, nor wish to. I have renounced my vows. A love for my beliefs made me leave. There was no other way forward. The gap between what was expected and what I could manage was too big. In early 2006, I met a man from Indonesia at the monastery. He's now both mentor and friend, and we share an emotional, if not physical, bond. It's difficult for someone my age to find relationships, or even sex, having become invisible. The world isn't kind to aging, especially if you have nothing to give in return. The upside is you can use that invisibility to do all kinds of inappropriate things."

Not elaborating any further, Rudolph blew on his cup and sipped his coffee.

"I'm picturing you as a child," I said. "You must have been born during the war."

"I lived on the outskirts of Nieuwegein, a municipality in Utrecht, but from a very young age, I was sure I had been put into the wrong family. Our parents kept photos of us as newborns in a brown padded photo album with *herinneringen* (which means memories) embossed in gold letters on the cover. I didn't look different from my three siblings. My eyes were the same colour as my mother's and I had a dimple like my grandfather. Indeed, most of my family said how much I resembled him. But I knew a terrible mistake had occurred. It was a sadness I didn't understand. From the age of five until my mother removed it when I was seven, I kept a small red vinyl bag packed at the foot of my bed, convinced that my genuine family would pick me up at any moment. I changed the contents occasionally to make sure I had clothing that fit me for my journey home. One morning, soon after my bag was confiscated, I fled with it to the nearest train station in the town of Houten, over an hour's walk away. Of course, a seven-year-old boy standing on the platform alone, waiting with a case for the next train, attracted attention. I couldn't explain to my parents why I disappeared. It has been a consistent theme in my life; from my arrest to my struggles as a monk, and especially to my time in America. I have always been an outsider and wonder if I do it on purpose. But it was the difference between what was expected and what I could bear."

"It has nothing to do with you. It's the world you've lived in."

"In that album," Rudolph said, "there was a photo of my grandfather holding me in the garden days after my birth. I still have it. The Netherlands had surrendered to the Nazis. It's June 1940, and he wears short sleeves. I'm swaddled like a mummy. Fields of potatoes and maize stretch beyond the yard under the sun, and he smiles with a familiar face I see in the mirror. My parents rarely discussed my grandfather, and I was just a child when he died in the spring of 1945. They treated him like a difficult neighbour, which he was. My grandparents lived behind our house in a cottage extension until his death, when my grandmother moved to Amsterdam and bought a small apartment here. My grandfather suffered emotionally in the war, and from my parents' limited accounts, he took the occupation personally. The war was hard for everyone, and very dangerous for some, but he blamed my parents, or their generation (according to them), and stopped speaking. He was an expert carver of wooden figurines and kept rabbits in the barn at the rear of the property near the end of his life. The carvings and animals multiplied, distressing my grandmother. My grandfather often wandered the back roads of the surrounding villages and footpaths between the nearby farms mumbling to himself, behaviour blamed on the invasion, which most members of my family both refused to speak about and never reconciled. My mother said my grandfather barely acknowledged them in those final years except for the occasional grunt, and made no small talk, retreating into a private world that he refused to share with anyone. I think I understand him now. He couldn't bear the idea of reliving his generation's suffering in the First World War, so he withdrew. It's a reasonable conclusion, I admit."

"Sometimes the mind can't handle more misfortune," I said. "The cupboard is full."

"Did you know your grandparents?"

"My gran lost her husband in the war and never remarried," I said. "She was an avid motorcyclist in her youth, living before I was born with a woman named Edith, a celebrated artist, until she moved out one year and into a hospital, which, over twenty years later, my parents discussed in hushed tones in other rooms, only saying with pinched voices that Edith had been poorly. I also have a memory of one photo of my grandfather, on Gran's sideboard in a pewter frame of engraved roses. In it he stood, half smiling or caught in open-mouthed surprise, hands in pockets, on a grassy slope beside a hedgerow to the left, breezily favouring one leg, in light-coloured pleated trousers and a short-sleeved dress shirt. His thinning hair, still dark, was combed straight back from his forehead, and behind him little clouds billow against a bright summer sky. The photo must have been snapped as he turned his head, settling into position, distracted by a sudden sound off-camera, or maybe by a bird crossing the horizon, but the effect, no doubt unintended, was to smoothen his face, and render him somewhat ageless. I remember the image so well because of the flaw, not despite it."

Rudolph held my hand until orange sunlight covered our faces. He suggested a leisurely walk back to the train station. Leaving the café, we turned toward the water and walked along the canal, past two rainbow benches and a pink granite triangle set flush into the front square of Westerkerk Church, with another raised above the ground ten metres away.

"The Homomonument is dedicated to homosexuals persecuted and murdered by the Nazis," he said. "Three triangles joined by a straight line of the same stone, all different heights."

Rudolph led me over to the raised monument, then turned and followed the line of granite to the canal's edge, where another triangle with four wide steps led to the water.

"There are many outdoor parties here. I enjoy watching the young people, dancing and laughing. No one notices I'm there. The last one went until five in the morning, and I had work the next day."

We crossed the bridge and walked another block, past small boutiques under an ornate iron and concrete portico that stretched the entire side of the street.

"I have reclaimed one clear memory of my grandfather," he said, "from the night of his death. There were rumours of Canadian soldiers advancing on our town; it was all anyone discussed. I entered their cottage from the rear door of our house late in the evening after sneaking downstairs. My grandfather sat in a chair in the dark by the window with his back to me, facing the glow of the barn lights, his arms hanging at his sides. From behind, I assumed he was asleep, as his head drooped to the right. I approached quietly, not wanting to disturb him. As I crept near the chair, he turned around, entranced, and when I touched him on the arm, his mouth twisted open, and he whispered to me that the pain was almost over. I looked outside, terrified. He had left the barn door and the hutch doors inside wide open. The rabbits had escaped, dozens hopping toward the fields, disappearing into the darkness and boom of artillery fire, with a few sitting dazed and immobile on the gravel drive in the amber light. In the 'hunger winter' of 1944–45, rabbits not caught in the crossfire would be captured and eaten. I ran to my room, locking the door. That night, my grandfather walked out into the dark, straight into the shelling. Later, in middle age, I dreamt of it many times, but didn't associate those scenes with my childhood until the conversations with my daughter — images of animals blown to bits in the wake of advancing battalions from the south. Blood, fur, and bone, thick and glutinous up close, frozen into the black mud. From a great height I flew over the remains, like rotting nightshades in the fields, with the corpses of soldiers scattered around, and nothing but the silence of all the dead under the moonlight."

At the next bridge, we turned right and wandered along Herengracht, one of Rudolph's favourite streets in the city centre, through dappled light from the elm trees that lined the canal, peeking into the dimly lit parlours of the townhouses. Except for the occasional decorative transom above a door or a window box filled with flowers, the exteriors were unadorned. Billows of pink clouds raced low overhead in the brisk, moaning North Sea wind.

"On evenings such as these," he said, "I'm taken back to winters in the Himalayas. A phenomenon occurs at great heights called a 'winterline.' Dust and smog rise from the plains below and form a second horizon at dusk, changing one's perception of the earth. It's almost a way of seeing, then seeing again."

The flat of his widowed grandmother, Marie, was on Herengracht, he explained to me, on the second floor of a corner building at Huidenstraat, number 356, with a Juliet balcony she often left open overlooking the barges and rowboats moored on the eastern side of the canal that she sketched and painted in the flood of morning light.

"The living room smelled of turpentine," he said, "was grand and bright, with high ceilings and tall windows, and doubled as an art studio. I loved staying for weekends and school breaks, watching her in an orange smock at an easel by the front window, or at the sculpting table, hands in gloves of dry, cracking clay, the white walls plastered with drawings and the wooden floors splashed with colours."

"My grandmother was also an artist," I said, "in her own way. She made folk art from scavenged items, refuse that covered the coastline where she lived. I almost killed her once as a kid. She was working in her narrow allotment she shared with the block of neighbours, painting a mural on the front gate in cheery shades of yellow, and I snuck up on her from behind, edging closer through the barley grass in complete silence, like a cat. In my head, I pictured jumping up onto her waist, as I did when I was small, both of us falling to the ground in fits of laughter, but when I grabbed her, screaming, I gave her such a shock she flung the paintbrush into the air and had a heart attack. Luckily, she survived, but lapsed into dementia, poor and abandoned, when I was still young."

Rudolph leaned on the canal railing, straining to look up.

"Marie was a sculptor in her final years. In fact, she blossomed both personally and professionally in her last decade and took to urban living immediately. It was as if country life cloaked her in a grey veil she removed in the city. She became fearless and had an affair with a well-known painter named Hendrik Jan Wolter, who lived in a ground-floor studio on the same block, which was quite scandalous in the 1940s. They stayed together, on and off, until his death in 1952."

"As my gran aged," I said, "she retreated from the world, holed up in a tiny bedsit on the upper floor of a council estate in Silksworth, a luxe-sounding name for one of the most destitute areas in the north of England. Her only excursions were to barren, fog-filled beaches on the Seaham coast to collect coloured glass, polished from years in the crashing seas, which washed up as refuse, with slags, solvents, and other by-products, from the furnaces of industrial iron and steel factories along the shores of Northumberland. Awed by this treasure, I watched her press the sapphire, ruby, and emerald jewels into the sides of disused clay pots she plastered in epoxy, then hold them up to the light like chalices. As the years passed, her flat smelled of vomit and NIVEA Creme. On our infrequent family visits, about which my parents complained bitterly, we would find her sitting by the speckled kitchen window in an apron-dress clutching her shoulders, a green tin of Heinz baked beans on the foldaway table, its top cut halfway open and pried back, her lower lip moving mysteriously. My parents' faces were layered with revulsion. During our last visit, she sat motionless in the parlour, a bunched-up tissue dangling from the left cuff of her blouse like ectoplasm, staring at the bare wall, a sage having at last left their body, the rotting shell of which had taken root in the carpeting, to be removed from the flat with the old furniture and discarded, along with her pots of precious gems, at the Lynemouth Colliery landfill. Years later, Lynemouth made the news. Acute coastal erosion had exposed blackened pipes, cables, and hosing from a century of Scotch mining along the shoreline. It was as if the ground just refused to comply. Black tentacles curved around the rebar on the television like dead snakes, pushing up from the pits where they were buried with impunity, the earth rejecting their foreignness as a body would a splinter on the ball of its foot. Watching those images, and that objection, I recognized my grandmother's resilience, and my own. It was how I'd felt my entire life."

"We discovered Marie and Hendrik once, my mother and I," Rudolph said, "in flagrante, when Marie had the date of our arrival wrong by a day and we walked into the bedroom in the middle of the afternoon. My mother was terribly upset, but I was thrilled. After Marie's death in 1961, this studio became the commercial office of a hat factory. As a law student, I stared up into the rooms right at this spot, leaning as far back as possible, searching for a trace of her, but fluorescent lights had been installed on the ceiling, the beige walls were bare, and the balcony door remained closed, its window blind pulled. I never went up again but imagined faded spots of violet or vermillion in the corners of the floorboards."

I climbed on the lower rung of the railing and stood up to look in the window, holding on to his shoulder to keep my balance, but saw nothing but a curtain of haze, and jumped down.

"In 2001," I said, "a few years before we met, during a research trip to the Royal Archives at Windsor Castle, something strange happened to me. Henry and I went to see an exhibit of a French photographer I admired, Édouard Baldus, and in the main hall a well-preserved platinum print was on display from 1900 of the Duke of York in the front passenger seat beside the driver of an early Panhard and Levassor autocar. Two older men sat in the rear while family members stood to their right at the arched entrance to a Gothic mansion. The woman in front, the head of the house, wore an embroidered day dress, her expression blurred by movement and not depth of field, because the frozen faces of the sisters, uncles, or cousins around her were clear. The driver was a statuesque young man in a full-length motoring jacket, ghostlike in the way he stared blankly ahead, and the typewritten card underneath read 'Photograph of the Honourable Charles Stewart Rolls.' I'd found that very name on a statue en route to France after I got out of that terrible hospital, the same trip that led me here. The description said that the photo was taken out-side the family estate, The Hendre, which I later visited in Monmouthshire, and that C.S. Rolls co-founded the Rolls-Royce luxury motor car company in 1904, made the inaugural double-crossing of the English Channel in June 1910, and died that same summer in a powered aircraft accident at thirty-two, the first Briton to be killed while doing so. So armed with the name, I went to the National Art Library in the Victoria and Albert Museum one late afternoon, at the top of a grand staircase off the Central Hall. There, I found lots of references, indeed entire books, dedicated to the sculptor of Rolls's statue in Dover, the Baroness Kennet, Kathleen Scott, which coincidentally was my mother's maiden name. I had zero knowledge about my family's background. They were dead by then, and I hadn't spoken to them since the 1970s. The library had a flatness to its light, as if the walls and panelling absorbed the day, leaving behind a constant dusk. Out of the leaden windows on the upper floor overlooking the inner quadrangle, I saw an old man in a grey overcoat strolling clockwise around the courtyard, chattering to himself as he walked in cir-cles. As the day faded, a gull swooped low across the green, hovered briefly below my window, then swiftly vanished above my head. I grabbed a final book from the pile on the study table, bathed in the last sunlight, published just a decade before — *Kathleen Scott: The Sculptor as Medallist*, and I discovered that Lady Kennet was born Edith Agnes Kathleen Bruce in 1878, and Edith had died of leukemia at St. Mary's Hospital, London, in July 1947."

As we walked out into Dam Square from behind the Royal Palace, three teenagers in bulky coats huddled on the street corner. I wasn't sure if they were praying or coming down.

"I wish I could have rescued my grandmother," I said. "Sometimes you find true kin within your own family, but they're erased for fear of contaminating the children."

"It's terrible when you can't save someone you love," Rudolph said. "When it's completely out of your control."

We followed the tram tracks that snaked through the crowded, noisy shopping streets out toward the North Sea Canal.

"My boyfriend, Paul, died in Los Angeles," he said. "It was a Friday evening. I had never seen such grace before, so I asked him to go — he was halfway to the other side, and to let me handle the terrible things to come. Following instructions, I placed Paul in three body bags — one zipper facing up, the second down, and the third zipper up again, with Paul wrapped tightly in clingfilm, including his face. But both the funeral home and ambulance refused to come. I drove around with him on the back seat, but couldn't find a place that would take him, so I placed him in the basement. We found someone who agreed to cremate him for twenty thousand dollars in cash up front, after hours on the weekend. I gave the last of my life savings to a shift worker at two a.m. on Sunday at the rear loading dock of a crematorium. No papers, pick up the box alone, left beside the garbage bin. Others were worse off, with no money. And no basement. The silence was a relief; the torment had ended. I was grateful for that moment, only the hum of night, maggots, flies, and pale smoke rising from the incinerator above me."

Rudolph and I said goodbye outside Centraal Station, heavy with rush-hour pedestrian traffic. Although more brittle, I couldn't help but feel Rudolph's state of mind was fuller and grounded. Swooping black-headed gulls made figure eights in the air above us, with two more fighting for a french fry covered in sauce on the pavement by an overflowing bin. Both our paths were journeys through such stations; anonymous and temporary, without an end point in space or time. We promised to meet when we were in the same city. Rudolph went to go, but I held him back, leaned in, and kissed him affectionately. Afterward, he cupped my face, and I felt his hands trembling. As he receded into the crowds entering the concourse, I recalled his words about the limits of what we can bear, and an image flashed through my mind, so sharp that for a moment I wondered whether I hadn't seen a photograph before, perhaps one of many taken of child evacuees in the Second World War, of a serious, quiet boy in high-waisted wool shorts, a pressed collared shirt, white socks, and school sandals, standing alone and defiant on an open-air train platform, hands at his sides and a small valise at his feet, determined to find his true family; a similar bag to the one Rudolph carried now, over sixty years later, as he passed out of sight into the terminal.

ANOTHER FIVE YEARS HAD PASSED. AT MONTGOMERY Station in Brussels in late September 2013, I alighted from the subway car and saw Rudolph waiting at the far end of the platform. He walked toward me in the breeze as the train sped away, and I recognized that familiar in-toeing on his left side, which had become more pronounced. Now in his seventies, Rudolph's face had slackened with age, his forehead marked by deep furrows, and his teeth more prominent by receding gums. We embraced, and his neck smelled of scented soap. Rudolph's white hair had grown out wavy and was combed back. He wore a tailored black wool overcoat and a smart grey cashmere scarf knotted over a dark sweater. I was passing through Brussels on my way to Paris and he invited me to stay for the weekend. He lived in a lovely nineteenth-century Georgian flat on Rue des Atrébates with arched windows and high ceilings. The apartment was near his work, and its small back garden blossomed with drooping English ivy and hazel. After storing my bags in the guest room, he made a reservation at Restaurant Adrienne, a nearby bistro. Rudolph seemed more introspective and spoke with a heavier voice, which I attributed to his age. After I freshened up and changed, we strolled along the cobblestoned street arm-in-arm.

The intimate restaurant was on the ground floor of a beaux-arts building, and we took seats in the back corner. The room was crowded but not loud, with muffled voices and a pleasant concerto wafting above the table. Rudolph shifted gingerly into the banquette against the wall, his arms supporting the weight of his body. I offered to change seats, then asked whether he needed any help, which he waved away with an upturned eyebrow, a smile, and a shake of the head, gliding in with one last movement. Threadlike blood vessels in his cheeks gave them a blush and, though thinner in the shoulders, he felt as limber as ever, he explained, ordering for us both.

"I slowed my consultancy work at the European Commission," he said, "and fear I have overstayed my welcome again, but it's my habit. It was important to stay through the summer, what with the Syrian refugee crisis. Once that is finished, I'm retiring and have thoughts of selling my apartment and moving on. The friend I spoke of on our last visit still lives in Amsterdam. Our relationship changed into a kinship of sorts, and I see him as a brother. It brings me joy to say I have a family at this late stage of life. My daughter is dead. After her surgery, she never had another violent episode, and gained weight, so it was successful according to the doctors, but she had incontinence and decreased initiative and went into a deep melancholia. She asked to be euthanized in the Netherlands, which was approved in the winter of 2010, just before Christmas, giving us the opportunity to choose a date together. At her urging, we chose her mother's birthday, the tenth of February. During those eight weeks, she was in good spirits, and didn't mention it again, which I found unbearable, until one afternoon she asked what her death had to do with me. I couldn't respond, shocked by the question, but she told me I had done everything possible, that she knew how much I had sacrificed, but that none of it was in my power. With one exception — she requested a Buddhist funeral. All she wanted in return was that I forgive myself. We had stumbled from one terrible decision to another. The whole wretched situation hit me. So I did. When the time came, she was made comfortable. I chanted the dying prayer from *Liberation Through Hearing During the Intermediate State*, what you know as *The Tibetan Book of the Dead*, and asked that she wasn't to be moved. I washed and dressed her body, and my friend joined me for four days as we performed the rites to guide her to the in-between. In one passage, we say, 'Now you have arrived at what is called death. You are transitioning to the beyond. You are not alone; it happens to everyone. Avoid attachment and insistence on this life. Though you may be attached and insist, you cannot stay.' The words became clearer in meaning as I spoke them, after leaving the monkhood, and after what she had said."

We left the restaurant, walking along the quaint side streets of Etterbeek to the Parc du Cinquantenaire. Once through its imposing arches, we strolled through the manicured gardens and sat on a bench under the spotlights by a long parcel of red, white, and yellow tulips. The trees had lost most of their foliage. Delicate branches reached up into the clear night sky like webs of spreading fungus on black earth. Rudolph gestured back to the gate.

"Here we have a ridiculous and garish monument to colonial genocide," he said, "conceived by King Leopold II, who of course was the owner of the Congo Free State, a vicious play on words, to commemorate Belgian independence from the Kingdom of the Netherlands under his father. Even now, bones belonging to the ten million Congolese murdered in the pogrom still emerge from the exposed roots of recently logged forests, along with shards of rubber they were forced to harvest. The entire country was one large concentration camp. There's an infamous photograph by Alice Seeley Harris from 1904. An emaciated man sits on the step of a local mission bent over two oblong stones,

which on closer inspection are one hand and one foot severed from his five-year-old daughter by militia from the
Anglo-Belgian India Rubber Company for failing to meet
his quota that day. Every soldier in the Force Publique
collected a limb for each failed quota. The Monument to
the Belgian Pioneers in the Congo is on the right, past the
fountains and hedgerows. It resembles a giant crypt and
honours those same gendarmeries for bringing 'civilization'
to Africa."

"It's a wonder people haven't torn it down stone by stone
with their bare hands," I said. "The lie is so enormous."

"Perhaps the size of the lie is why it remains untouched."

We turned back toward the arches and saw the lights
of a neoclassical building that formed the southern wing
of the grand arcade, which Rudolph explained was the
Cinquantenaire Museum, free to the public on Friday
nights. We walked into an airy nineteenth-century double-
height foyer. Phthalo-green wrought-iron pillars and girders encircled an upper balcony. Gothic cloisters held fine
European silverware, tapestries, and altarpieces from the
baroque period to the present. Entire wings housed exten-
sive collections from the ancient Americas, including an ar-
ray of artifacts from the Maya, Aztec, and Inca civilizations,
Mochica ceramics from Peru, the world's oldest Inuit kayak,
an Olmec terracotta figure from El Zapotal, and a massive,
six-tonne stone totem from the Franco-Belgian expedition

to Easter Island in the 1930s. Time didn't allow a visit to the Near Eastern, Southeast Asian, or Egyptian galleries, but we wandered through winter light from the transom windows in the Islamic Art wing, coming to a set of stairs that led to a peristyle room containing a perfectly preserved Roman mosaic from Apamea, Syria. Up another stairway, we emerged into the Grand Colonnade of Civilization, the centrepiece of the building. On a marble plinth at the end of the mammoth hall stood a giant bronze statue of the emperor Septimius Severus in an angelic pose, his hand reaching out over the mezzanine.

"As you have noticed," Rudolph said, "it's impossible to see the museum's entire collection in one visit, being nearly the size of the Louvre, bursting with antiquities stolen from the world's great civilizations and fetishized by curation."

The longer he spoke, the more he raised his voice, and people turned around.

"Stripped of their setting, reduced to random objects, removed from their environment. Baroque sculptor Paolo Naldini found this impressive statue in seventeenth-century Rome, missing its head and outspread hand, and began a restoration. The bronze now stands intact, as you can see. Note the sandal's ankle bands, the creases in the simple robe, his weight on his right hip, the left leg limp to the side, with the restored right hand extended in a benediction or warning. We should remove the hand and leave his outstretched stump, headless, ankles in what could be shackles, one leg dragging behind him, with a plaque honouring the slaves who built modern Belgium."

A guard approached and spoke to Rudolph in French, telling us to get going and stop making a fuss. We left the museum and returned to his apartment, shuffling past the crowds on Avenue de Tervueren under an inky-black sky. He said I could stay in his room, but it was my decision. Like anyone coming out of the closet, he was apprehensive, excited, and winced as we kissed. Sometimes he laughed when he held me. When Rudolph fell asleep, I spooned him and recalled our first meeting those many years before. I had walked around the upper hall of Namgyal Monastery, which was open to the public at certain hours, the morning after our hike. Peering into the window of the main temple, I hoped to catch sight of him through the bars, nervously scanning the backs of the robed monks sitting inside but felt self-conscious to be looking and stepped back. Novitiates passed with a smile, none making me in any way uncomfortable. My misgivings were unfounded, yet I couldn't shake the sense of intrusion on something forbidden.

On my last morning in Brussels, after another night together, I asked Rudolph if he was happy — a question he found difficult to answer. There are many accomplished violinists, he explained, yet few play in a philharmonic. It doesn't temper their passion for music. Rudolph sought perfection, to be reunited with the All. Despite a lifetime of study, he remained uncertain about what awaited him. There lay his folly, his fall from grace. The closer he came to the centre, the more he was repelled. The nothingness at the core of everything, the empty random awe, held no peace for him, only turmoil. He feared becoming a small, solitary figure again, a child alone with his terror. This was a feature of quantum mathematics, he explained, that only chaos exists in the marrow.

"Perhaps I should have been a mathematician instead," he said. "Only death will show if I'm wrong. I ask your pardon, as always. The irony isn't lost on me that I tried everything to avoid death all these years. Many years ago, you asked me what I was running from. You never told me what you were running from."

"Abandonment," I said. "A long time ago, I stopped running. I was betrayed and institutionalized. I've felt hunted ever since. Put another way, you could say I'm running from the hunter. Packs are harder to kill than strays."

We moved outside and sat in the garden with my bag at the door.

"His name was Jan Koopman," Rudolph said.

"Who is that?"

"The young man I followed into the woods who first arrested me. It wasn't difficult to access my criminal file and find his name once I was a lawyer. And it was easy to locate him. He was a police officer for forty years, married and childless, living at the same address his whole life. I drove to his home in Haarlem many times over the decades, sometimes parking for hours, but never knocked on the door, although I followed him once to a local bar and sat at a table a few metres away, observing his movements."

"You didn't hurt him, did you?"

"My monastic robes may be soiled, but I haven't lost my mind. His wife would often garden out the front of their house in the mornings, planting delicate flowers, her hands covered in soil, until ten years ago, when I saw Jan holding her arm as she hobbled along the road with a cane, always staring up at the sky, pointing at nothing with a bandaged hand."

"Did you ever confront him?"

Rudolph shook his head.

"I went one last time a few years ago. His wife's skin was bruised. She was very thin and had on a bicycle helmet and cheap silk slippers. Jan held on to her tightly, and they both looked quite dishevelled. I got out of the car and went to his side. Jan asked me if I could assist getting his wife through the front gate and was nothing but grateful to me for the help. When he finally manoeuvred her up the path and through the door, he turned and waved. I started the car and sat there for a few more minutes, weeping. And then drove away."

He put his hands together and brought them to his trembling lips.

"It's like a fog has cleared," he said. "It doesn't make me happier, but anger gives me meaning."

"I trust your anger," I said. "Don't let anyone dissuade you from it or tell you otherwise. Anger saved us from extinction."

"I still have two souls in my body. The one I nourished, and the one I starved. They don't overlap. Half of me haunts the other half. The soul I starved, I starved slowly. But I wasn't running from danger; I was running from power. I shouldn't have hesitated. Instead of waiting on that platform as a child, I should have kept on walking and never turned back."

IN NOVEMBER 2016, GLORIA EMAILED THAT RUDOLPH had gone missing in Bali the previous summer and hadn't been heard from for three months. His social media feeds, email address, and cellphone had been deleted or were offline. The last sighting was on a humid August morning in Ubud an hour after dawn, walking past a popular café on Jalan Raya, the main street running through the centre, heading east out of town. Rudolph's trail went dark, his credit cards and bank accounts remained open but unused, and there were no leads as to his whereabouts. He had opened a small business in Ubud in 2014 with his friend Premananda, which failed and had closed. Rudolph's lawyer there had put his affairs in order, according to the message I received from Gloria. When I got through to her on a video call, she explained that the land and building were sold a few weeks before he vanished and the funds redirected to his estate lawyer in Brussels.

"Rudy told his Indonesian lawyer he wouldn't need his services again once the transfer was complete. The Brussels lawyer contacted me because I'm listed as the executor of the will. Although he isn't presumed dead, the lawyer thought it wise to confirm my details in case his status as a missing person changed. I'll keep in touch with any updates. Would you like me to pass along your contact information to the Brussels lawyer if he receives any news or if you play any role in the estate?"

"But I won't be named in the will," I said. "Although we were confidantes, Rudolph has far closer friends."

Anxious as to his whereabouts and condition, especially considering his instructions when firing his Balinese lawyer, which seemed to rule out foul play, I knew wherever Rudolph went, he went in sound mind but not heart.

My last email from Rudolph was in early April 2016, four months before he vanished. In it, he says nothing of his troubles. The message is only a few lines. I became accustomed to hearing from him in snippets and spurts. Often he sent what amounted to a haiku. At seventy-six years old, time no doubt moved differently, undulating rather than moving in a straight line. Even going in circles. It reads, "I am watching dozens of white herons following a tractor across the rice field. Sometimes they overtake it and double back, likely for the worms."

Rudolph's decomposed body was finally recovered on December 5 by the Karangasem Search and Rescue team. It was spotted by a French tourist expedition to Mount Agung in northeastern Bali, twenty metres down a ravine very near the peak. I can't say what became of his soul after he fell. He may have been halfway to the other side when he left town that August day, determined to keep going this time. Rudolph's goal was the summit, but perhaps his uneven gait caused him to slip on a treacherous part of the trail. His left leg had broken cleanly at the knee, and his wrist, hip, and neck had suffered compound fractures. Three separate units were deployed throughout the day of retrieval. The recovery mission took fifteen hours due to the position where he lay. Because of the sacred nature of Mount Agung, the removal of Rudolph's body wasn't by stretcher; he was carried down, under the guidance of a local elder, who always ensured the torso was level with the knees. Cleansing ceremonies were held in the community. Premananda permitted them to cremate his body under

Hindu custom. Since his daughter and ex-wife were both deceased, his ashes were given to Gloria.

On a bracing January day one month later, Gloria and I returned to that same beach just outside Los Angeles where they had secretly scattered Paul's ashes almost thirty years before, which was an arduous journey for an eighty-three-year-old to undertake halfway around the world.

"How soon the darkness comes," she said. "The brevity of a human life; the ceaseless hours and days and years, and at the end of it you look up and say, 'Where did the time go? How have I reached the end so quickly?'"

We stood side by side in the gusts of wind, relics out of time, like two aliens from some distant planet, as couples holding hands strolled by and people walked their dogs, and watched as Rudolph's remains drifted into the Pacific.

CHAPTER FOUR

JOHANN LUND

On the day of our London reunion in late October 2019, I stood outside Johann's stock-brick townhouse on Beaufort Street in Chelsea. I had received a message from a mutual friend in Montreal that he had misplaced my contact information and was too preoccupied to find my email address or phone number. Although we had been in touch once or twice, it had been thirty years almost to the month since our last meeting, and I had no idea he lived in the U.K. Johann had been diagnosed with an aggressive form of Parkinson's disease and found typing difficult, but in a few days a warm email appeared in my inbox using bold twenty-four font asking that

I visit him. Age and circumstance, along with a reluctance to embrace the digital era, kept us adrift from each other until I received his message.

I was buzzed through the red door with a dragonfly knocker and aluminum blinds on the glass, pausing alongside a long black radiator and tall silver-framed mirror to collect myself before ascending the worn oak treads to Johann's flat. Before I had the chance to knock, he opened the door and stood shaking before me, now seventy-seven, sporting the same spectacles and moustache, gleaming white along with his hair, very cropped, wearing an Oxford shirt and a crocheted brown cardigan. He had the same alert, green eyes of his youth and the same gold hoop in his right ear. Grinning, Johann put his hands on my shoulders and squeezed.

"It's like no time has passed," I said.

"Speak for yourself. Look at the state of me."

After a breakdown in the early 1990s, Johann had recuperated at his family home near Odense on the island of Funen in Denmark. We planned a reunion there in 1994, but he cancelled at the last minute. A blue airmail letter sent special delivery described the Gothic brick cathedrals, cobbled streets, and graded row houses in the old town where everything seemed built in miniature, to the windmills and hedgerows that dot the northern coastline where he walked alone through hectares of forest bordering the farmlands and coastal meadows that stretched out to meet an empty sea.

Johann wrote that, although physically fit, he was "unwell in his head" and pleaded for a postponement. Of course, I obliged, remembering my long convalescence.

I embraced him tentatively, not knowing the extent of his discomfort. He led me through the foyer and the open kitchen to his expansive study glowing in the sunlight, lined with stuffed bookcases and a threadbare Persian rug. The study's casement windows overlooked the narrow back garden Johann shared with two other tenants: a fine art appraiser in his sixties from Lyon, and a Slovenian mathematician, now with a grown daughter, who fled Yugoslavia for London after the purges of the early 1970s, who assisted with his care. There was talk of exchanging apartments when Johann had trouble with stairs.

"I've lived here since the late 1990s. We're across the road from Denis Charles Pratt's one-room bedsit at number 129, better known as Quentin Crisp, until he abandoned England for America in 1981. So the queer bona fides are impeccable."

After sitting him in one of two high-backed club chairs, I went to fill the kettle, finding a blue-and-green-striped tea cozy covering the porcelain teapot. The kitchen was immaculate, but the washer was full of files and papers.

"Where do you do the laundry?"

"My housemates provide meals and fresh linen, and there's no longer any need to change the bedding more than once every two weeks. Nothing happens in there anymore to call for it, trust me. But I worry my illness may bring incontinence soon, and about the pressure I'll put on my friends. Come sit with me for a while."

Johann had progressive supranuclear palsy, which advanced faster than other forms of the disease. Both his hands shook, his right significantly.

"I now masturbate without consciously moving my hand. Always focus on the positives."

"Have they given you a prognosis?"

"With the correct medication and therapy, I can ward off the worst symptoms for another few months, then my balance, sight, and mental faculties will diminish."

He exuded the same intellectual command, more professorial now, his voice lighter and raspier than I remembered, but with the same flat Canadian accent, its phonation hardened from speaking Danish as a child. He had shrunk a few sizes with age, as if air had escaped from a nozzle. Yet he still possessed a presence, someone who turned heads when talking.

"Soon the Christmas lights will go up in the vestibule," Johann said. "Ivana never misses a year, and they stay up from the first of November to early February if you can believe it, to include both calendars, ours and the Eastern Orthodox, including Candlemas, but I know Slovenians celebrate Christmas in December so it's just a ruse to keep them up for as long as possible. For such a scientific mind, she indulges in magic. Ivana thinks because I'm vaguely

Catholic in some suspicious way I won't care, and I don't begrudge her decorative indulgences to be honest. Anything with colour and life these days. You should see her flat come December. It's like a clown threw up in there. But she makes a mean potica. The house fills with the smell of laurel, thyme, and rosemary. I thought she would want to return to her homeland, even just once for posterity, but she has no curiosity about her country, harbouring neither good nor ill will, considers it a place someone she doesn't recognize lived in, no less a stranger as someone she once passed at a traffic light, and will never go back. And to my knowledge, she never has. Now Ivana's daughter is family. I much prefer her as an adult, of course, having zero interest in being a father of any kind, as you know, but I always treated her as a colleague of sorts, barring the occasional fancy dress. The state drilled into me that starting a family was illegal, and I obliged with a middle finger. She came to our marches, often screaming the loudest, and had no inhibitions."

"Remember how difficult it was to get people to raise their voices? Canadians are so very well-mannered," I said.

"I saw her to school and roared with approval when she rebelled," he said. "I bought her first whistle and showed her how to make her body go limp when being arrested. She was only nine, but it didn't faze her."

"How lucky to have someone so no-nonsense to guide her through adolescence."

"And she's such a fine person now. She organizes my support and leads my care team, just like we used to do. The binders and dividers, daily notes, checklists, and scheduling. Point people and bridging new members, medication dispensation, clinical trial forms, pain management, powers of attorney, and when to call no-code. The mundane details of planning a death."

"Do you remember the head of immunology at the Jewish General Hospital always said, 'It's not the death, it's the administration'?"

"Truer words were never spoken. I dare say all that practice has made a tremendous difference as I navigate this final chapter. The lessons are the same for the old and young, except for the injustice."

As I took his hand in mine, the worst of the shaking subsided.

"I'm content to go," he said, "as I've been weary of life lately. It's harder to find my place these days, and I can't imagine wanting to stay much longer. To have lived long when others died before even falling in love. I can still offer encouragement and answer questions, which won't always be the case. After almost eighty years, I will finally die. I'm doubtful I left this world in any better shape. Indeed, in my life's work, I fear I have failed. Admittedly, I often feel lost, like there's no space for me anymore. The world I knew appears quaint from this angle. It's the civic violence that worries me the most, greased by the wheels of technology. And if there's one thing in history our people recognize, it's violence."

"To think that fascists used to have to mail pitiful little periodicals in plain brown paper envelopes," I said, "excited if their subscriptions passed a few hundred."

"Were we so wrong about the future?"

"Yuri recognized it first. He always focused on immediate impact, not grand achievements."

"That's why you fell in love with him."

My lip trembled, even after thirty years. "So, you knew."

His head spasmed while glancing out the window, so he rested it against the brown leather wing of the chair. "Yuri sought me out late one evening at the house, very anxious, and asked if we could talk. He was in a state; so overcome with guilt that his very presence in your life hurt you so deeply, and didn't know who else to turn to, poor dear. I asked him to tell me everything. He was horrified that he was breaking your heart piece by tiny piece, because he couldn't love you the same way you loved him. Goodness what a kerfuffle! And all over two people who were so committed to each other, just in different ways. It broke my own weathered and bitter heart, I must admit. I said you of all people knew what you were doing, and that if platonic love was enough for you, then he should trust you. But he still had doubts. So I asked him (because heaven knows that was our default back then) if he discovered that he only had a year to live, would he leave you, or would he stay by your side? It didn't take him more than a split second to respond. He would stay with you, come what may. Then he asked what to do if he woke up in three hundred and sixty-six days and he was still alive? We giggled like schoolgirls, and I put my arms around him and told him he had a bonus year, and to choose whether he would do it all again. Sadly, he found out about his illness shortly after. So you see, it became all too real, as it happened."

The sun streamed in squares across the floor from the windows, then dimmed just as abruptly as clouds passed overhead.

"At some point it stopped mattering that he didn't love me that way," I said. "Eventually, it had nothing to do with him. My devotion was unconditional. He would've eventually chosen someone else for his affection. But it doesn't change a thing. I chose him. I'd do the same again."

My voice trailed off. I cleared the cups and asked if I could do anything else for him.

"Yes," he said, "you can return tomorrow for another chat. I'd love your company."

"How's your reading?"

"I still manage."

"I'd like to bring something for you. A testament of sorts. One final witnessing."

I cancelled a planned visit to East Kent the following day with my partner, Sam. As I walked out into the afternoon glare, my breathing slowed from the heavy heat hanging in the air so late in the season, I wasn't upset about the last-minute change of plans. Indeed, I looked forward to the disruption.

THE NEXT MORNING, I SAT AT JOHANN'S SIDE AGAIN, A journal I had brought with me and two cups of passion flower tea between us on the coffee table.

Johann paused and attempted to bring the cup to his lips, but it spilled. I rushed to help him, pulling my chair closer, and dabbed his chin dry.

"About six months ago," he said, "just as I experienced the first symptoms of my illness, I opened a litre of semi-skimmed milk and doubled over at the counter in the kitchen to catch my breath as I peered at the side of the carton. Hana Kato's photo stared back at me after all these decades, heavily pixelated. An analogue image run through dozens of computer programs, with a number to call for the Missing People charity, like a faint signal from space. Upon this strange discovery, I went to the charity's website and its Help Us Find page, scrolling late one evening through hundreds of photos of the disappeared from across the U.K. and the Commonwealth: London, West Midlands, Yorkshire-Humberside, Eire, Northern Ireland, Nigeria, Canada, New Zealand. There were grown men, old people, young women, children of every age, faded photos from decades ago, and digital ones just taken. I wandered through this random and incoherent collage of the recent and long vanished and recall one selfie of a male teenager in a hooded sweatshirt in front of the new building still under construction at 8 Bishopsgate. Beside it was a blurry Kodachrome photograph, most likely from an old Instamatic camera, of another sweet, smiling girl with a bright pink mohawk in a green leather jacket, taken somewhere along the southern coast in the 1980s. On one side, there was pasture; on the other, a blue haze of sea against a pale sky."

I leaned in. "What did the photo say? About the girl?"

"Only 'Southeast,' so perhaps it was Kent or East Sussex, but I recall it vividly because the shy, sweet smiles of the girl in that photo and Hana were so similar, and a shiver went up my spine for all the lost. As I loaded more and more pages, an overwhelming sensation took hold of me, a repulsion mixed with despair."

I poured him another tea and helped him finish a brioche, which smelled of burnt cinnamon and rose water.

"On the table is the diary of our journey," I said. "I haven't looked at it in a long time. Rereading it for me was like a traveller returning to a place hoping to relive an experience of great significance but finding everything changed. I came close to destroying it, and don't wish to feel that pain again. Hopefully, it will be of interest."

JOHANN WAS SITTING COMFORTABLY IN THE STUDY, THE
diary closed on his lap, when I returned from shopping
for the weekly supplies. The afternoon light streamed in
again, concealing his face and casting long shadows over
the floorboards. I asked if he was in pain, but he shook
his head. I made him ginger tea, returning with a tray of
fresh cups and saucers.

"You must be wondering why I asked you to read it," I
said, "and in truth, I'm not entirely sure. Like Yuri and me,
you were always on the move, headed in another direction.
Restless."

"But I was, shall we say, a careful traveller. Not nervous
exactly, but I needed a schedule, a plan of some sort. Perhaps
it's because we are foreigners of everywhere. When you are
history's barbarians, every empire seals its gate. We become
accustomed to the in-between, the liminal spaces. You once
came to me in Montreal, dismayed that the International
Socialists kicked you out of a meeting."

"I remember," I said. "They saw our sexuality as a
bourgeois construct, a decadent tool of oppression against
Marxism, and asked me to leave. No one was kicking the
door down in the Cold War. It was like being shunned by the
least popular group in high school."

"Our people are stateless," he said. "We're born in every
country and yet can call nowhere home. This statelessness
remains in the mind and affects the wandering body. It

burrows within. Travel reminds us of our exile, but for a short time frees us from our burden. A celebration and a mourning in tandem. Admittedly, it does become exhausting to always be the guests, never the hosts. Our fates rest on the permit of others, most often withheld, grudgingly granted, and easily revoked. A knife-edge on which we all balance."

"I can't fathom trying to conjure Yuri for anyone who hadn't met him," I said.

Johann asked me to put drops in his eyes. The loss of muscle function led to a lack of blinking, which dried them out and made it hard for them to work together, sometimes giving him double vision.

"You were one of my first teachers," I said. "A rarity in those years. I was still a child, another terrified kid with no mentor to guide me through the destruction. All our oral traditions, cleaved. You were already a man, intelligent and fearless, and full of passion and ability. Infatuation followed."

"*Now* you tell me."

"But you were so preoccupied. So broken by grief. I clung to the idea of you more than anything, already being in love. You held the knowledge I was desperate to learn, and our histories never put to paper. I hoped to be like you — to steal the way you moved through the world. I was still trying on lifestyles like jeans in a mall."

"It's strange reading about Karl, Yuri's German boy-friend," he said. "Through Karl, Yuri was introduced to people who would later lead the German Green Party, including a close association with Jörg Zink, a founder of the Peace and Ecology movement, who coincidentally once came to visit me here in London in the early noughts while at a conference. He spoke of them both."

A gauzy light settled over the study. Evening traded places with the day. I made a dinner of baked salmon and a bright green salad, and once we finished, took Johann on a walk down the stairs through Ivana's flat and into the pleasant temperature of the garden at dusk. After sitting him in one of the ornate iron chairs with a couple of thick pillows and a throw blanket over his shoulders, I pointed out the early constellations of Pegasus, Aquarius, and Pisces in the southern sky, and a red-hued star I didn't know in the east, beside the faint glow of the Andromeda galaxy rising as night fell. He swallowed his medication with a hit of wine from a large goblet brought by Ivana.

"Being grateful for small things isn't a bad way to live," he said. "Even so, to be unbroken a while longer would have been nice. Did you know Yuri would never leave Khazar?"

"No. I convinced myself that as long as we kept moving, we bought time," I said, "and Yuri would never die. We could keep going indefinitely. My guard was down. Of course, that's the moment death finds you."

I looked up at the stars and tried to picture an auroral glow from a solar storm, fires churning in a leaden sky, then opened the diary and read to Johann.

> *I judged time by the moon, brushing a cloth dipped in rosewater, a memory of bloom, for weeks across his sunken chest, down his serrated shins, and over the flabs of skin hanging from them that used to be his calves. His lips retreated past his gums, his eyes drifted in space. Pain was his last private thing. I could only guess the meaning of his moans as I touched him. Angry mounds of glands exploded in his groin and deep in the caves of his underarms. Everything was pale — the white fire, the adobe, the blinding day, his cracked skin, his bleached, swollen tongue. I longed for the scurry of mice or the bark of a dog. The single bird outside, the size of a swallow, made no sound, its belly like Yuri's hair, the colour of ash.*
>
> *The sweats and cough devoured his flesh, and pneumonia overwhelmed his lungs so that he drowned in his own phlegm. I gave him the antibiotics until it was obvious they weren't helping, and with a tender shake of*

the head, he refused even the paracetamol. My
mind raced. Outside was a dune I swore had
not been there before. Murtaza, Hassan, and
Parviz helped me take care of him until the
last day. I fashioned diapers from towels and
brought in the vinyl outdoor chaise for him
to lie on after explaining to them that Yuri's
body would shed its fluids, then asked them to
leave me alone with him after his eyes glazed
over and it was clear his gravelly breathing
would soon stop. Yuri's rasp was drowned out
by the wind screaming through the open win-
dow. I wondered if he heard it from wher-
ever he had gone, entranced by the pureness of
its sound, or waiting for its violence to pass.
The next morning, after staying up all night
with him, I went to the bathroom. When I
returned, I suspected he was dead but waited
until I was sure. A strange emptiness filled the
moment as I sat there. I wanted it to be pro-
found, but it wasn't.

I put down the diary and pulled the throw, which was falling off his shoulders, across Johann's chest.

"The boys were so present. Hassan chose cremation for Yuri instead of a traditional Tower of Silence, where his ancestors would have left the body on a platform to be picked clean by vultures. Since the vulture population had been decimated in central Asia, modern Zoroastrians favoured fire, using immolation to eliminate the corpse, which had no value in death. The government forbade cremation, so add that to the list of prohibited activities taking place in Khazar in 1989."

With my help, Johann took another sip of brandy and closed his eyes, as if remembering something comforting.

"Hassan explained after death, the soul lingers on earth for three days," I said, "when its deeds in life are judged. I cleaned the room and took the towels and Yuri's clothes out to the desert and buried them myself, then washed his body and wrapped it in muslin, and together we burned it in the morning sun on a rocky dais we built from Burjan stones on the crest of a low dune, changing to dust in front of me, letting the wind take Yuri's ashes where it may. The possibilities were endless. We drove to our favourite spot, interring his bones as deep in the earth as we could, which took most of the day."

"And what happened to you after?"

"Hassan arranged for another driver to take me as far as Tabriz, where Bahoz was waiting. I left most of Yuri's money with Murtaza to buy his next village, only taking what I needed to get me home. From Turkey, I returned to Europe, and to a spectacular new world. The Berlin Wall had fallen while I was gone, and the Soviet Union was dissolving."

Darkness descended on the back garden. I helped Johann take another sip and asked if he wished to rest. He shook his head. Thinking it was just a tremor, I asked again. He said no but preferred to return to the library due to the fading light. I helped him up and we said goodnight to Ivana, taking the stairs slowly. After settling him into his chair, I turned on the side lamps and brought him a cognac and water, and a double for myself. Before I sat down, he asked me to bring the entire bottle. With both hands, he sipped from the snifter as I held his right wrist.

"Honestly," I said, "I doubt if Yuri's insurance was ever collected. There was no corpse or record of death, and I never returned to Canada."

"And what of Khazar?"

"I hear from Murtaza and Hassan occasionally, but less as time passes. They're well, and Murtaza renovated his guest house across the street. He's doing a good business, which the three men run, and they named the restaurant in the courtyard Yuri's Place. So far, they've evaded the authorities."

He chuckled, and I held on to his right hand to stop the trembling.

"The failure of grief lies in its inability to revive the dead," I said. "It bellows at the same time as it whimpers. Yet it changes nothing. We grieve all the more because we grieve in vain. It's no use explaining Yuri's death in any more detail to someone like you. What could I add that we both haven't

experienced countless times? Writing more down seemed un-
necessary, like saying the sky is blue."

Johann reached for the snifter and drained the balloon
glass, his shaking finger pointing to the bottle.

"In dreams I've seen Yuri lately," I said, "but he never
speaks or looks my way, always too far away to address, like
a ghost, already dead, a vision within a vision. He sits at the
farthest table from me in a dim bistro ignoring his drink,
and I try to get through the increasing crowd, or he turns
the corner off a busy pedestrian avenue in the early evening
and melts into the long shadows, and when I reach the spot,
there's no side street. Or I'm taking a flight of stairs and
glimpse him on the landing above, gazing up at something.
My gait is slow and laboured. When I scream to him and
reach the top, he's moved again, yet I keep shrieking, unable
to escape the stairwell, wondering why he's dead or didn't
notice me."

I poured Johann a generous refill as he pointed to the
window. "Such is the nature of dreams," he said. "The question never answered, the sense of never arriving, the un-
named abyss at the centre. They will scatter my ashes there,
under the alder out back."

"I'd have liked to scatter Yuri's ashes," I said, "in a garden under a tree somewhere, wherever they eventually scatter
mine, so that we could have been together, but that was never
meant to be. Not in this life, Johann, or any other."

CHAPTER FIVE

FRANK MERTON-WOOD

I n early May 2025, I drove eastward out of the village of
Maussane-les-Alpilles on the Route de Mouriès in late
afternoon light, past hectares of silver-green olive fields
stretching up to meet the low mountains of the Chaîne
des Alpilles, their arid limestone cliffs curving across Les
Baux-de-Provence from the Rhône to the alluvial Plaine
de la Crau, to le Moulin Gris, an eighteenth-century mill
that had been converted into a boarding house, where I
would finish my research for a series of lectures I was to
give on Édouard Baldus's early photography in Burgundy,
Dauphiné, and Provence, originally commissioned by the

Le Comité historique des arts et monuments in 1851. I turned right at the signs for the Mas de Fauchon auberge and a winery whose name had so faded from the sunlight that I couldn't read it, passing a high grey iron gate on my left and a narrow, stony plain on my right that led to my home for the next two months: a rambling farmhouse with Grecian blue shutters and at least two separate wings I could make out from the gravel drive. From there, in front of me, stood the flat stone front and gabled roof of the largest wing, accessed through steel trellises covered in dense creepers. The building stretched back the length of the property. A large garden of ornamental grasses and rose bushes fronted a Roman aqueduct that, like the house, continued to the rear fence. Two more annexes enclosed the courtyard, their walls hidden behind waves of vine and clusters of bright purple climbing flowers. Expansive beds framed in bleached timber of cascading feathery rosemary, lavender, succulent, and wild thyme bordered the front walk on both sides. Wide stone steps led to a heavy wood and brass door, which was open. Excited finches and house sparrows welcomed me, circling a crumbling chimney stack perched near the edge of the terracotta-tiled roof. I saw groups of birds nestled in the deep crannies between the stones just below the roofline where the ancient plaster had eroded, leaving thick, rambling cracks of indeterminate hazard.

I was met by my hosts and taken on a tour of the farmhouse, appointed with mid-century upholstered sofas, cobalt glass vases, art deco lamps in abstract shapes, a long, stainless-steel bureau with curved edges and burnished gold legs, and a carved refectory dining table abutting a large communal kitchen with white cupboards and a stained oak island. They showed me to my quarters upstairs. Two rattan chairs with cream cushions were placed on either side of the open picture window overlooking the interior flower garden, a small iron desk and high-backed chair stood against the stucco wall to the right of the door, and a double bed to my left had built-in alcove shelves. Grouped on a mantel opposite were asymmetrical ceramic bowls in bold reds, blues, and yellows. A space heater was provided in case of cool, windy evenings, which were common into the spring in this climate, they explained, where pale skies and intense sun often gave way to clear and cold starry nights. In fact, the winds were gathering strength when I arrived. I heard a violent whooshing of trees and whiffed something perfumed, but gazing out onto the atrium I didn't see any trees at all, likely due to the labyrinthine nature of the house's sections, just the thrashing of poppies, lavender, and fiery bougainvillea, which made little sound. The world was mismatched and unreal. Noise piped in for effect, a soundtrack with no discernible source. I recalled the story of Huguette Clark, a wealthy heiress and recluse who, for no reason anyone understood, voluntarily spent the last half of her life in a small, sterile room as a paid resident of the Doctors Hospital on the Upper East Side of Manhattan, while her various mansions and estates purchased in the early decades of the twentieth century remained empty but meticulously maintained as time capsules, at considerable cost, by a coterie of staff acting on her instructions, including the cars in the garage with licence plates from the 1940s. She possessed an estate valued at over three hundred million dollars. The single memento she requested from her former life was a tape recording of the ocean from the state rooms of Bellosguardo, her sprawling twenty-three-acre manor on the Pacific coast in Santa Barbara, costing forty thousand dollars a month in upkeep, and which she had not stepped foot in since 1951. Refreshed after a shower and a dinner of fresh bread, green olive tapenade, rillettes, and heritage tomatoes bought en route at the village market, I settled in for the evening. The interior garden was near the roadside, judging from the rumble of a passing car competing with the roar of the gale. The moon was a few days from full, so the courtyard and flora glowed silver-blue from my chair by the window. I awoke in the middle of the night from a loud crack. Startled, I listened for the sound but heard only the moaning wind. Feeling chilled, I rushed to the bed and pulled the duvet over my head without taking off my house clothes. The windowpane vibrated violently, the glass creaking as it juddered against the force of the storm, and I thought of the sea.

WALKING OUT TO THE VERANDA BELOW MY ROOM THE next morning, half asleep, I found a dead swallow on the step. The noise in the night was the bird smashing into the window. I wrapped the tiny jet-black carcass in a paper napkin and buried it in the garden under a cluster of fragrant oregano. The sun was high, with no clouds in sight, and the wind continued to blow wildly. I walked into town for supplies instead of driving. On the other side of the road, behind a tall wall, I could see the second floor and gabled roof of a stone manor house, its olive-green shutters closed except for one, surrounded by conical cypress trees and a wide, commanding plane tree well over thirty metres in height. The wind's boom through its branches was what I had heard the evening prior. In the piercing sunlight, the house glowed the palest pink. I strolled past the entranceway, and the iron gate was now open. Sneaking a peek inside the compound, I saw a slight, elderly man standing motionless, hunched over and facing away from me at the gnarly base of the tree. He wore a collared shirt with the sleeves rolled up to the elbow, braces that crossed his back, and tweed trousers. I thought he might blow away, but he remained still until I approached with a hello, then turned and waved at me like an old friend.

"I think I've been here a while," he said, raising his voice over the clamour, "but can't be sure as the gale is so hypnotic one loses track of time. It's the most incredible sound, the rush of the mistral through this tree. Close your eyes — it sounds like standing behind a giant waterfall. One never tires of it and yet one never fully gets used to it. The sound has driven some to madness. Mistral storms are otherworldly, arriving in cycles over the weeks of spring, then vanishing, replaced by complete stillness. That's why I try to get my fill before it leaves, because once gone, one can't quite remember the fury, like a dream forgotten upon waking that felt familiar. Oh dear, I sound like William Burroughs. My apologies, I'm Frank Merton-Wood. Won't you come inside? It's time for my almond-pistachio torte, I made it this morning, and warm prune brandy."

I introduced myself and explained that I boarded across the road, which he said was splendid. Frank was short, his brown skin was streaked with even darker liver spots, and he spoke with a posh American accent. His coarse grey hair was thinning, revealing his skull in a certain light, but his copper-brown eyes sparkled with life. The skin on his face was taut, and his cheeks were severely sunken and gaunt. He had lost the fat around his temples, which made his jaw look much wider than it was. Frank's smile was warm and generous, and he gave off a wonderful cordial energy. The door was wide open, which by then I assumed was commonplace. He touched my arm, patted me on the back, and gestured for me to head inside.

The foyer had a cloistered ceiling, and the stone walls and floors had been left in their natural condition. The damaged double parlour to the right was papered in peeling red damask. Two baroque-style armchairs painted gold with burgundy upholstery were opposite a plush but tattered cream sofa with oversize cushions. Thick, pistachio-coloured velvet drapes covered the side windows, and an ornate eighteenth-century writing desk sat underneath rows of framed drawings on tawny paper. Simple white diaphanous curtains that had rust stains running in zigzags from top to bottom fluttered over the front window. Frayed books of every imaginable size were stacked in piles on the dusty floors, along with clusters of knick-knacks: glass and copper vases, brass collection plates, pewter pomander balls, wicker baskets, iron bells, rolls of fabric, and a group of small dark bronze statues. A broken pearl nautilus chalice stood alone on the floor in the corner. The table lamps were on despite the sunlight streaming in. Frank gestured toward the air above the furniture.

"I entertain in here," he said, "but lately there are few new arrivals, and now it's often parties for one, along with whatever old ghosts are floating about. None of it is in great shape anymore, but everything has a purpose. I throw items out constantly, I assure you, even if it looks otherwise. The attic is overflowing, although most of it is in disrepair, but I can no longer get up there to see for myself, being the chipped and weathered fey-looking gnome one spies with sympathy in an untended garden."

Frank explained he had osteopenia (which he described as the stage before osteoporosis) in his ankles and hips, so he rarely climbed any ladders or steep steps.

"The dangerous part is coming down," he said, "so I'll be fine as long as I stay up. Truth be told, I don't feel safe on any moving apparatus anymore, like bicycles, motorbikes, or skis, which is a shame, because I was a decent roller skater in my day. Backward crosscuts and forward rolls, shoot the duck, even one or two spins in my arsenal. A few easy single jumps launching from the rubber stopper on the front of the toe. Nothing fancy. I reckon I still have them in a box somewhere, probably packed beside my silk shorty-shorts, the ones with the side piping and the tiny slits, and my many see-through tank tops, along with my moustache."

A noise came from the back of the house, and Frank led me into a bright drawing room.

"Come, Dusty," he said, "special delivery. Fresh blood. A gentleman caller!"

Large-form silvery paintings of Provençal fields, poppies, almond trees, and forest passageways, unframed, hung on the walls alongside charcoal drawings of empty rooms, unoccupied chairs, and narrow corridors. Three freshly painted Impressionist-style works in oil were taped up in the sunny corner opposite the window. The room contained only a baby grand piano and an old phonograph on a table against the wall. Two piles of oversize coloured pillows covered the floor. Through the rear double door-way, I saw wood cabinets and a long granite counter and heard the opening and closing of drawers. A trim, smiling man with curly silver hair, untamed grey eyebrows, and rimmed spectacles came through the door wearing a loose linen shirt, matching slacks, and well-worn brown leather slippers open at the heel, holding out his hand. His lenses were incredibly thick and magnified his eyeballs so much he looked like he had Graves' disease.

"Hello there," he said. "Did you come in the post?"

"This is Oliver," Frank said, taking the man's arm, "but everyone calls him Dusty. Can you believe we used to be the same height? And now I'm at least three inches shorter, if not more. And counting, I'm afraid. We're the pairs of cypresses in Van Gogh's paintings, the stunted one leaning on the taller. Dusty is the grandson of a famous violinist in late nineteenth-century Avignon, and an accomplished pianist in his own right. He's blind as a bat now but can play almost any symphony from recollection. Even though he retired to Morocco and lives there permanently these days, I get him up here often with various bribes. You name it, I've promised it."

Frank patted the piano. "Plus, of course, free play on my Érard. And unlimited wine. Dusty came up for my seventieth birthday, which falls a week after Eurovision in Basel at the end of the month. It should be quite a banger, even if it's just us. We would love to make it three if you can join us. Let's have that brandy, and the cake is ready."

"I am going into town to pick up groceries," Dusty said.

"It's slightly nerve-wracking," Frank said, "since he cannot really see. He drives like Mister Magoo, but insists on going, and always promises to go extra gentle on the blind turns."

We exchanged a few words, and I explained I was staying across the road. As we said goodbye, Dusty turned around.

"Hope to see you again. Do come back."

"It's a date," I said. "I'd love to hear you play."

He was very charming, with a relaxed demeanour, a person whom nothing fazes, and raised his eyebrows every time he grinned, especially in response to Frank speaking, which, with his bulging eyes, gave him the look of being in a constant state of surprise.

Frank and I walked out the back with our drinks. He showed me his dry garden, maintenance-free, as he could no longer tend to it, full of desert flowering plants, drought-resistant herbs, prickly pear, and barrel cacti of different sizes. The plot ran the length of the rear yard in front of a long, low outbuilding open to the elements, with the same terra-cotta roof and no doors, filled with ancient rusted manual farming machinery, placed as if curated under the rows of rail ties: rotary hoes, combines, and plows. One resembled a giant Victorian tricycle.

"Like most things here," Frank said, "they have outlasted their usefulness, but I can't bring myself to ask a scrap dealer to remove them. I can't bear the thought of them being dismantled, shredded, and melted down. And so they exist out of time."

"It's like an art museum."

"Each piece is so different; they are almost sculptures. Like the winds in this region, each has its own personality. They are old friends. The mistral today comes from the northwest and is incredibly strong and butch; the levant from the east is very humid, a complete drama queen; the tramontane is a dry, icy wind from the north, totally bitchy; the marin is a warm, moist south wind from the Gulf of Lion and very sexy, and the Saharan sirocco blows in from the southeast, a real screamer, all red dust and blustery rain."

We walked to a gravel drive that turned into a patio-stone path. The brandy tasted sweet and burned my throat. Beyond a leaning wire fence, a dense forest fronted rolling hills under a sky of ombre blue. The wind moaned and the stones crunched beneath our feet.

"I'm trying to place your accent," I said.

"British American, so I speak with a softer lilt than other Americans. People have a hard time pinpointing where I'm from. It was worse with my French lover, who was older and born in this very house, but he grew up in the English midlands during the war years, Provence by way of Shropshire, so his accent was positively wacky."

Near a row of dark cypress stood a tree I didn't recognize with unusually shaped pale leaves. Frank took a sip of brandy, gesticulating to the tree.

"Oh, this is my pride and joy. It's a ginkgo biloba, originally from China, but of course one finds them all over the world now. They are living fossils. The greater species are two hundred and ninety million years old, real spunky, and withstood the dinosaur extinction. It possesses motile sperm, and the female doesn't produce cones, so I know this tree is a male. From a distance it looks hairy, but up close one can see the delicate fan-like leaves in the shape of lily pads. They mimic the umbrella pine, which has no foliage until the very top, when it opens like a parasol, easily the most unusual tree in this area, though most are found closer to the coast. The ginkgo was one of the few organisms to survive the Hiroshima atomic bomb. Six survived in the epicentre of the blast zone. The Japanese have a word for the trees that survived the atom bombs — *hibakujumoku*. Astounding. The leaves turn a beautiful saffron in autumn. Of course, ginkgo is a medicinal treatment for all kinds of ailments, but especially for neurological conditions, memory improvement, stuff of that nature, and as a supplement it was given for dementia, though I don't know if it's still approved for such things. Maybe I should eat the leaves myself."

"Fads come and go, don't they? One minute it's a cure and the next it's a carcinogen."

"Once, a long time ago," he said, "I was given extremely large doses of it on the recommendation of some healer, an acolyte of that nutcase Louise Hay; nothing but an unguent hawker who had us chewing on a few spinach leaves as we withered away because we didn't love ourselves enough. I believe now one calls them a wellness guru. Ten bitter horse pills a day until I had internal bleeding, heart palpitations, gallbladder swelling, and anemia. I broke out in rivers of blisters, the whole nine yards."

Frank stroked the rough and knotty bark. "Ah," he said, "we humans love a miracle."

We returned to the back garden and sat at a small iron table sheltered from the winds, the top inlaid with jade decorative tiles that Dusty had brought from Morocco in their "shipping years," as Frank called them, pouring us another brandy, when wooden crates of all shapes and sizes from Agadir on container ships to Marseille showed up on the doorstep, full of traditional blue and white porcelain plates, clay tagine pots, ceramic tureens, steel couscoussieres, pewter water dispensers, lemonwood spoons, hand-painted ochre platters, djellabas in every colour, sequined Berber wedding blankets, and bolsters made of fine cactus silk.

"It was lovely," Frank said, "as the house had been mine for some time but was still almost empty after a decade. Dusty was determined to fill in the vacant spaces. The physical ones, anyway."

"How did you end up living here alone?"

"My lover Charles died in 1989. It belonged to his family. They were wealthy and influential and had cut him off long before. I don't know what they thought worse — that his lover was Black or was a man. Charles was the last surviving member, so there was no dispute over the estate. But he died before he could return, so the house was bequeathed to me, a devoted friend of two decades, according to the probate. We were warned against mocking the law by calling me something more appropriate, or it would be held up for years, or challenged outright. The state could be so cruel. Both our deaths were preordained. I was supposed to go next. Certainly, there were near misses and close calls. I did a countdown. Two years, one year, six months. Then, by a stroke of fate, I didn't die. I've lived here ever since, in these peeling rooms, under these lovely squat little mountains, ravaged as I am. Time passed, and new medications were discovered to manage my illness. The toll on my body by then was significant. In fact, it might soon be hard to distinguish me from the furniture. Eventually I will disappear into the tableaux. Someone may try to sit on me one day or put me in the garage, begrimed and petrified, gradually oxidizing to the colour of the plants, with a permanent view of the agave and agapanthus, as well as the silver slopes. That would be something indeed. But you must join us for dinner tomorrow evening if you aren't engaged. Dusty is making a daube. Bring nothing. We have it covered. I have a landline in the kitchen. I can give you the number, but I rarely use it. Who is there to call? Ring me if you need anything, but better yet just drop by, day or night. I don't stand on formality; the door is always open. That way, it's a fun surprise."

THE NEXT MORNING, I RECEIVED A BLACK-AND-WHITE postcard at the Moulin of a nineteenth-century woman in a light-coloured day dress, her long tresses pulled back in plaits, languishing against a lectern. I turned it over and an ink stamp at the top said CARTE DE VISITE, and under it was written, "Looking forward to dinner tonight, come by anytime. Frank MW." There was no postage attached, so had been dropped off in person. I arrived at five o'clock with a Poire Williams eau-de-vie I had found at the end of a row of shelves in the village grocery. It was another picturesque sunny afternoon and dollops of fluffy clouds moved in unison across the sky. When I walked into the kitchen, which

smelled of oregano and roasted meat, Frank was dressed in
a flowing swath of deep green velvet with gold tassels hanging off the neck, and he wore a Napoleonic bicorn chapeau
with a tall purple plume feather. He was so diminutive that
he drowned in the outfit, resembling a small child who had
raided his parents' clothes closet. Dusty had on a white nun's
wimple and a black embroidered caftan. Frank ran over and
put a floppy, blood-red Victorian ladies' hat on my head,
adorned with brindled feathers and a bright orange chenille
ornament in the front, and a Tyrolean green felt riding cape
over my shoulders.

"The pages have been slow poisoned with arsenic," he
said, "and the courtiers of Elke Sommer have gathered
to anoint a new sovereign. The Holy Sister of the Cool
Lakes arrives to bestow a deadly kiss and bless the corona-
tion. Nancy Reagan, the Gravedigger, is hovering uselessly
from a distance as usual, and I stand as the Gold Stick-
in-the-mud-in-Waiting to protect the crown, the Count
of Monte Crisco!"

We dined that night on a salty pissaladière baked with
anchovies and fresh herbs, tomato-olive salad, Dusty's
famous daube, which filled the room with the scent of
cinnamon and cloves, a creamy gratin dauphinois, a thick
slice of oozing Brie de Meaux served with sliced apples,
and sweet calissons with candied melon. And, as promised,
plenty of wine. Frank had taken his velvet drape off the

curtain rail in the bedroom and fashioned it into a cape, and when he became too fatigued from its weight to keep it on, we traded outfits.

"Where did your penchant for costumes come from?"

"The Sisters of Perpetual Indulgence," he said. "Nuns in full habit doing direct action on roller skates? They were a convent after my heart! That's where Dusty's wimple was made. Charles was a member of the London Order for years, but they've changed their name to the House of Common Sluts."

In cavernous rooms surrounded by such high stone walls we resembled, it seemed to me, inmates of a remote tubercular asylum, our X-rays deteriorating, where we could dress up for our passion plays in the twilight hours as an alternative to upping our laudanum. We danced freestyle in the parlour to disco hits played on an old phonograph: "Free Man" by South Shore Commission, "I Was Born This Way" by Valentino, "Cherchez La Femme" by Dr. Buzzard's Original Savannah Band, "Got to Be Real" by Cheryl Lynn, "Is It All Over My Face" by Loose Joints, and "Transformation" by Nona Hendryx. At one point, Frank retrieved fans from a bijou trunk in the back corner and we started fan dancing, waving them over and around our churning bodies. The real pros, he explained, could fan dance with huge handkerchiefs and often toured Europe and across North America. Frank regaled us with stories of going to the Trocadero Transfer, or the "Troc," as he called it, in San Francisco in the late summer of 1978.

"After dancing all night," he said, "on the way home, a large group of our friends climbed the grassy knolls of Corona Heights Park to its sandy, barren top. The light happened upon us like a developing, illimitable photograph, while the fog retreated, anticipating the coming sun, and the world lay in wait. Edges changed first, the grading of soft blue outlines like the future unfolding before us. The flat, grey rooftops of a thousand tiny apartment buildings below stretching to a crowded bar graph of skyscrapers across Union Square and the serrations of the Diablo mountain range beyond the bay. Steps made of sawn logs snaked up to where we sat on the rocky outcrop, clumps of moss clung to crevices in the rock, and red dirt dusted our white trainers. That we had only seen a handful of dawns was bewildering. It occurred every single day as we slept, but to witness it was as rare as an eclipse. We made drunken promises to never miss another daybreak, to reunite on this hilltop, to never be alone again. From the peak, arm in arm in the hot wind, we watched the sun spill over the city and the Twin Peaks, with red-tailed hawks hovering nearby, the sounds of the jays, chickadees, and nuthatches for company, and dreamed of all the days and days to come."

THE FIRST TIME I FOUND FRANK INCAPACITATED WAS
the morning after our dinner. I passed the gate and popped
in to say hello, discovering him on the gravel drive. He
lay on his side in a semi-curled position, his head resting
on his right arm, which extended straight out from under
him. I thought he was asleep, but he had a glazed, hypnotic
look, as if staring at something lodged between the tiny
stones. Frank didn't respond immediately. Indeed, it took a
few tries before I roused him. He came to, apologizing as I
pulled him up and led him back to the house. By the time I
helped him up the stairs and into bed, he had regained his
former vigour, saying he had become lost in thought and
found time passing strangely. Upstairs, the bedrooms were
simple, adorned with a few sketches on the walls and worn
area rugs under the bed frames. No people were present in
any of the etchings, line drawings, or oil paintings. Nor
were there any photographs. His bedroom walls, like most
of the house, were bare stone, but the encroaching damp
from the decaying roof had meant covering certain sections
in a clear plastic casing.

"I know what you're thinking," he said.

"You do?"

"Uh-huh. It looks like I live in a colostomy bag, but since
I do nothing here anymore except sleep, I take little notice."

There were more dinners and nights of abandon over the
following weeks. Frank would emerge as a Bohemian aunt

in a billowing takshita and turban, passing out drinks in crystal digestif glasses before dinner, or as a German lieutenant in First World War regalia, ladling soupe au pistou from a hand-painted tureen in a brass button tunic and wool trousers. Frank's zest was infectious. It rubbed off like pollen onto those around him. I became hopelessly, fatally besotted. Most afternoons were spent beside the piano, where Dusty played nocturnes by Fauré and barcarolles by Chopin. There was an inexplicable presence inside the house, an unknown source of air circulation. A ghost in the machine, impossible to ignore. Even with everything sealed, I saw curtains fluttering. The home possessed its own personality; a faded, merry grandeur in a supporting role to its owner.

THE GALLERY IN ARLES WAS TUCKED AWAY ON A RUN-down, unremarkable side street in the old town, off Rue Amédée Pichot, next to a beauty salon and a florist. With its plain brick exterior, it looked more like an entrance to an apartment building than the host of a travelling exhibition of nineteenth-century photography.

Frank entered and was struck silent. I watched him approach the first set of Baldus pictures with reverence, like a child having found a secret fairy door in the woods. The exhibit was split into three parts: surveys in the nearby towns of Nîmes and Orange, showcasing the strange beauty of decaying ancient Roman monuments; the juxtaposition of the untamed, barren landscape of Ollioules Gorge just outside Toulon and its decorative railway station made of iron, glass, and refined stone; and the devastating floods of 1856 in the lowlands surrounding Avignon and the city of Lyon, all in magnificent albumen silver print. Each photograph was devoid of people and almost apocalyptic in its scope. Frank looked at me with awe.

"The scale of these," he said, "with no fussy detail or formula. See the unobstructed clarity of the foreground? The poetry is in the balance of document and artistry, the invitation so direct it practically slaps you across the face."

Returning to the floods, Frank gestured for me and took hold of my hand. The woman with bleached hair behind the desk glanced up.

"Notice how the scene captures the influence of nature on the human-made environment, absent of any people," he said. "It's almost biblical. It feels like a destroyed civilization, not just a temporary calamity. All the same, they crumble. History and progress, up close, without a maker."

"He was ahead of his time," I said.

"By a century, I'd say, at least."

"Long ago, during an overnight stay in Paris with a young man, I was introduced to his work. Then, many years later, as an art-history student, I came across an album of the French railways he presented to Queen Victoria that remains on exhibit in Windsor Castle. The exhibit's accompanying passage on Baldus referred to a scandal only recently unearthed about his real identity. Eduard Baldus of Cologne, an expert printer, changed his name in 1835 to Édouard to escape detection. A warrant across Rhine Province had been issued for his arrest on counterfeiting charges. A photocopied section of the French warrant, which remained unserved, stated that under Article 139 of the penal code, the crime of forgery was punishable by death. Édouard Baldus escaped with his life. He absconded to Paris as a fugitive, arriving in 1838, no doubt at the Gare du Nord station, as that is where Cologne trains arrive, belonging nowhere, to begin again."

I held back tears and glanced at the still-staring woman. Frank let go of my hand, gracefully spun, circling the entire room, and returned to my side.

"Without people, some think there is a sense of lack," he said. "A hollowness. But it's the opposite. The empty spaces give the photos meaning, and it's the silences that have the most weight."

Frank gave me a giant kiss.

"Precisely," I said.

"Thank you for this gift. I want one of each for our walls. Now we can get our hair done and buy flowers, without even leaving the street!"

Frank turned to the woman at the desk and gestured grandly around the room. "What's not to love about this afternoon?"

THE DAY BEFORE THE EUROVISION FINALS, WE WERE SE-lecting costumes from past winning songs. Dusty had gone to Avignon overnight and asked me to choose something for him. Frank's favourite song was "Ding-a-Dong" by Teach-In from the Netherlands, which took the crown in 1975. He found a sheer crepe fabric with a bold floral pattern he fashioned into a flowing blouse. I chose "Save Your Kisses for Me" by Brotherhood of Man from 1976, which we both agreed had been an underwhelming winner, mainly because Dusty and I could be the singers Nicky and Sandra in a duet. After discovering two matching blue berets, I rummaged through a stack of boxes for black and white separates, which I could wear as a pantsuit, and discovered red silk pajamas for Dusty with wizard sleeves and a long tunic he could cinch at the waist using Frank's concho belt with a gold-plate buckle.

"I was wearing my cowboy drag the night I met Dusty in a backroom in New York in 1976," Frank said. "A real little sissy butch. You would have needed a butterfly net to catch me. And who doesn't love a Spanish heel?"

"Were you more passive or active?"

"I was the biggest bottom in San Francisco, and that's saying something. A total ponce. Who needs a hanky in their back right pocket? Amateurs, that's who. The bar had fashioned a dark room for a monthly one-nighter. I think for the rest of the month it was a chophouse, because I vaguely recall eating a rib-eye steak there."

"From one meat rack to another," I said.

"Thick black drapes were hung halfway across the area behind the bar, creating a more intimate space with the lights turned off. Very down-market. I was standing against the rear wall. Dusty sauntered past me and leaned against the curtain, thinking it was a wall, only to fall through, flooding the room with light. The men screamed and scattered like vampires."

"Such an auspicious beginning to a friendship."

"I literally picked Dusty up; first, off the floor; and second, to my apartment. He's the only survivor of my former life. The rest are gone. Extinct. The counting stops into the dozens. One gets thick-skinned. Germans have a wonderful word for it — *dickfelligkeit*. Soldiers used it in the Great War to describe coping under fire when everyone has fallen. Oh, get a perm for tonight! I wonder if the local coiffeuse in town can fit you in at the last minute. Dusty's hair is too baby-fine now to set a curl. Tell me about Sam."

"I was a war bride. He's fifteen years my junior. Missed the plague completely. He cruised me in a bakery at nine in the morning. Hungover, croissant in hand, I looked around to see who he was staring at. Turned out it was me. He was so gentle with my spirit, and so kind. Smart as a whip and prepared for my wounded heart. Suddenly, I was the elder. A repository of our stories and traditions. After we met, I went back to school."

That afternoon, I drove to the village to shop and returned to find the house empty. I looked for Frank in the garden then circled around to the front gate. The setting sun cast long shadows from the hedgerows across the drive. The stones had turned peach, the fields ochre, and the Moulin's shutters purple. I searched for him along the road before returning to search behind the house. Past the outbuildings was a wide field of ancient olive trees and no fence had been built to separate the two plots. Only a shallow, dry ditch running the length of the grove demarcated the properties. Beyond the trench, Frank stood still and in profile in the middle of the neighbour's field beside the twisted, warped trunk of a tree, staring up at the grey Alpilles under a pale waxing moon, his neck hump and curved back more pronounced. Hunched over in the rows of old trees, he could be mistaken for someone, perhaps on an outing from a local theatre school, trying to imitate their drooping pose. It looked as if he had petrified on the spot where he slumped. I walked out and gently took hold of Frank's arm. He gave me a confused look as we strolled back toward the house, the caked clumps of dry soil softly collapsing under our feet.

"Oh dear," he said, "I climbed up the hill for a view. It's so peaceful but not that high. Not high enough, I suspect. It won't do at all. One doesn't want to return to the valley. One wants to stay put to see the sunrise."

When Frank had rested and was cogent, I went to his bedside.

"I'm guessing this has been happening a lot. Do you know what's wrong?"

"It's encephalopathy," he said, "not so uncommon a brain malady if one lives long enough in such a deteriorated state. I've told Dusty. It was, I'm sure, the reason he wanted to come up. I wonder what parts of my memory will go first. I wish to God I could choose. Bye, shitty ex-boyfriend. Oh, and that closet-case that gave me penicillin-resistant chlamydia. It will take what pieces of the brain it wants, leaving me with the residue. It's been wonderful having you here these past few weeks."

Frank turned his head to the dusk as I stroked his arm.

"Truly," he said, "I could eye the sparrows for hours through this window, screeching and diving in circles across the garden, if I could suspend the fading light. But they leave so fast."

"These visions. What do they feel like?"

"Lately, I've had this feeling of being out of place, as if time has caught up to me. These episodes don't feel like dreams; they are more substantial than you in this room.

Rationally, I know they're hallucinations. But I have an over-whelming sense that, if I stay, I will die at the right time, an expression of my guilt, I suppose, at having survived. In today's vision, I walk along the street shirtless in dark jeans, holding a purple balloon on a string and knotted on my wrist is a braided band of ivory-coloured rope frayed at its edges. Charles is beside me. He has on his favourite denim coveralls over a white tank and is laughing. I see my reflection in the window of a café and my black hair is growing out into a fine afro. The sun is hot on my face and my right heel is stinging from newly purchased sneakers. When I reach for Charles's hand, I feel moisture on his palm. There is a smell of diesel, and I hear the tinny voice of a disc jockey coming from the car radio of a green Datsun stopped at the lights with its win-dows open. My keys are attached to a steel carabiner hooked to the loop of my jeans. There are faint sounds of horns and engines revving, and as we cross the street, a lady in a yellow sundress and jute sandals passes with her black dachshund. I dodge the leash and collide with a tall, tanned, bare-chested man with wild grey hair. He grabs my elbows, smiles, and disappears into the crowd. Though I cannot place the day, I remember the balloon so distinctly and feeling carefree and buoyant. It's the last time in my life I'm thinking about ab-solutely nothing. Not the past, nor the future."

He turned his face to me and squeezed my hand. "But it's strange. I don't remember ever wearing a wristband. You know, I was a librarian for most of my career. The library received one copy of all the periodicals. They were for reference and only for walk-ins, but when new issues arrived, we divided the old ones up between the staff and were free to bring them home. I loved to take art journals because I dreamed of being a painter. In *Artforum* magazine, I happened across an article that explained colour doesn't exist until inside someone; it's only a series of electrical signals sent from the eye cells to the brain, which vary from person to person. Colour doesn't inhabit the physical world; it exists only in the minds of its beholders. Everything is colourless until we show up. Isn't that marvellous? If no one is left to vouch for one's life, it's as if it never happened. Knowing I would die allowed me to keep living. One may only bury the past for so long. It surfaces again, and one returns to that first time the shovel broke cemetery ground, when we weren't aware of the cataclysm that, unbeknownst to anyone, had already settled on us like a fine dust. To think, later, I went to funerals where family members condemned the body lying in the coffin even while they drained the bank accounts dry. So embrace it. The dead are at our whim. We can choose to remember or forget them. Choose what parts to cherish, and what to discard. Or eventually, as I now see, the time will come when the parts are chosen for us."

I stayed the night in Dusty's bed to watch Frank, though for the rest of the evening and the next day he was

his old self, regaling me with stories of his celebrity crush-
es. Parker Stevenson, Eric from the Bay City Rollers, Sam
Melville, Rex Smith, Lloyd Haynes from *Room 222*, and
Lyle Waggoner and the Ernie Flatt Dancers on *The Carol
Burnett Show*. One of his biggest and longest-lasting was
Scotty Baldwin from *General Hospital*. He was incredulous
that neither Dusty nor I knew him, even though Frank
didn't know the actor's real name.

"Pearls before swine," he said, "both of you! Luke and
Laura's wedding was only the television event of the century. Scotty barged in with his on-again, off-again girlfriend,
Bobbie, who was Luke's sister and Laura's nemesis. Scotty,
who was always a little light in the loafers if you ask me,
caught the bouquet, contested his divorce from Laura, and
declared himself evil and unscrupulous. He became the fey,
underhanded district attorney of Port Charles, married Alan
Quartermaine's mistress for her money until she and Rick,
Laura's adoptive father, were murdered. Scotty pinned the
blame on Luke for Rick's murder when it was Laura who
killed them while suffering from amnesia."

It was dusk by the time we got dressed in our costumes.
The birdsong had faded and the light in the west was dying.
We set the table with jars full of cheerful yellow brooms and
cowslip picked from along the deep ditch that ran beside
the stony plain across the road. Frank served us grilled lamb
chops with delicate curved bones the size of tongs, a fragrant

aubergine gratin with thyme, marjoram, and basil from the garden, an entire board of chèvres scented with lavender, truffle, and peppercorns, and bowlfuls of ripe Carpentras strawberries with double cream. He checked to ensure the oven was off three times.

"This new affliction," he said, "will finally, after half a century of resistance, turn me into my mother, who was convinced everyone else in her family would leave the stove on, candles burning by the rayon curtains, the space heater plugged in overnight, or a year's worth of lint in the dryer filter, and burn us to smithereens. She checked the oven knobs day and night. To think I kept it at bay until now."

By midnight Saturday, once "Wasted Love" by JJ had taken the crown for Austria in the Basel finals, we had settled into the piles of pillows on the floor by the piano, and Frank asked Dusty and me if he could request a present for his birthday.

"With your permission, I want to paint your portrait tomorrow morning, weather permitting, out in the garden, before Dusty leaves for Avignon, as long as he promises to trim those Brooke Shields eyebrows."

Dusty straightened his back, balancing on the pillows, and saluted. "Yes, Way Bandy," he said.

Dusty was going on an overnight visit to see his sister. He reached out during visits to France, even though they weren't close. Whenever he had tried to speak of a friend's illness, or a current beau, she would change the subject or pretend she hadn't heard.

"I wish you could be in the painting," I said.

"Absolutely not," Frank said. "I'm already like Dorian Gray, thank you very much, except sadly, I'm the picture."

AFTER A SLEEP INTERRUPTED BY VAGUE DREAMS, AND A quick breakfast of reheated brioche and bitter coffee in the morning, I turned into the drive wearing a white overshirt to see Frank ready in a painter's smock and a striped boater hat, setting up his easel. Dusty, brows freshly trimmed, accompanied him, in white to match me, as instructed. It was three days until Frank's birthday, and he painted for well over six hours. We broke for a long lunch at noon and resumed in the mid-afternoon. The result was a delicate and Expressionist-style portrait, with broad strokes and an impasto finish. The colours burst with the yellows and oranges of the sunset. Pleased with the outcome, as were we, Frank hung it over the mantel in the drawing room beside the piano.

"It will serve a ceremonial as well as aesthetic purpose," he said to me. "Your official adoption. Dusty has already given his approval." Tears welled in my eyes. Finally, at the ripe age of fifty-nine, I had a father.

The following morning, I slept past breakfast. My host brought me another antique postcard from Frank, this time of a vintage funicular in Marseille taken from the roof of a building near its base with the tower of the Notre-Dame de la Garde basilica on the summit in the background, from what I thought to be the early 1900s, with the same ink stamp on the back, under which Frank had written, "Joined Dusty for the Avignon trip. Gone for the day and evening. Won't be long. Back tomorrow."

Dusty and I had planned a grand tagine for Frank's birthday in two days. Dusty would stop en route to pick everything up. With Frank now accompanying him, I was less concerned about him being alone for one of his spells, and it afforded me the surprise opportunity to do a trial run of his second gift: a trip up to Les Opies, the peak of the Alpilles, a pleasant beginner's hike I had been researching off the Route D'Arles just east of us near the town of Eyguières. We thought we could manage the shortened circuit of a few kilometres if Frank used a walking stick, as the ascent was described as gradual, with few obstacles, affording him the grandest view over the Plaine de la Crau. The twenty-two-year-old cashier at the village shop adored Frank, and was happy to be on call should we need a piggyback, but we withheld that from Frank lest he should (and he would) feign exhaustion just to be carried home by Bruno. We would pack a picnic basket filled with charcuterie, hard cheeses, and wine, and toast to a new decade. Costumes would be too challenging, but I had found, to my amazement, three pretzel headbands in metallic colours at the Wednesday flea market in the village, likely from a long-forgotten Jane Fonda workout.

Once Dusty returned to Morocco, depending on Frank's condition, I had been considering moving across the road to give Frank more support for the rest of my time in Provence. We had sat in the parlour early on Sunday morning, with the wind even stronger than the day we met.

"Please decline if you want to," I said, "but I wonder if you might want me to join you in the house."

Frank, gracious and composed, took my hand. "I'd love nothing more," he said, "as I fade (hopefully slowly) into this new twilight world, than for you to provide colour."

After lunch, I drove to the trail entrance west of Eyguières. A wide, well-kept path followed a grassy knoll along a stretch of vineyard with no hikers in sight. Streaks of high diaphanous clouds criss-crossed the route above the hill, and climbing the slope in the whooshing wind, pleased at the gradual gradient, I passed a lone umbrella pine over ten metres in height that Frank had mentioned on our first visit, its long trunk void of any leaves until the top, when delicate acacia-like branches burst into a billow of foliage. In fact, I thought the shape of the crown was like the tumescent cloud floating above it. The vegetation thinned out the higher I walked until rock replaced shrub. In no time I neared the crest of a steep forge, looking up at a small stone tower at the peak of Les Opies, likely an ancient shepherd's hut, with a pyramid roof that from this angle resembled a tiny, peaked hat. The trail grew steeper and thornier from there, posing a challenge for us with Frank. Still, a flat thicket led to the edge of the cliff, with the most magnificent vista across the Durance Valley below that stretched to the gently curving horizon. From that vantage point, the rind of the earth became clear. I was ready to stop running.

On the return drive, a super bloom of young poppies rippled along the roadside, so dense that the coverage turned the entire field orange, and I stopped to take a longer view. Driving past Frank's closed gate, I imagined a lifeless, empty house one day in the future, thought of the mistral sweeping across the Rhône Valley, then vanishing as if it had never come at all, and pulled into the Moulin. The wind boomed through dinner and growled against the window as I tried to sleep. Squalls of such strength they hit the walls like thunder. Barely a breeze remained when I awoke, but my hands trembled reaching for the kettle and a fullness in my ears lasted well through the morning. A temporary shift to the threshold of my hearing had occurred so that whenever someone spoke, the consonants disappeared, concentrating the vowels into a low drone in my head.

JUST BEFORE NOON, DUSTY APPEARED AT MY DOOR.
Wondering why Frank's gate was shut, he had come across
the road, assuming Frank was with me. Confused, I asked
him why Frank wasn't still with him in the car. Dusty explained he had gone on the trip alone.

We opened the gate. The front door was closed. Finding
the house empty, we walked out to the garden and found
Frank hanging from a noose knotted around one of the railway ties in the outbuilding, his back to us, facing toward
the machinery. The ladder stood on a diagonal near his feet.
Frank had kicked it away but likely couldn't push it over. Not
wanting to disturb the scene, we left him there until the authorities arrived but stayed with him. It was the worst thing
I have ever done. The day was still, with no wind. I wouldn't
have had the courage to leave him there swinging. As the
hour passed, I recalled standing on Les Opies and wondered
if Frank was already dead, or if I could have saved him had
I returned earlier and stopped at the house. The thought of
Frank up there alone in the roaring gale through the night
froze me, and I forced the image from my mind.

Dusty and I buried Frank's ashes under the ginkgo tree in
the festive box that had contained the cake for his birthday.
Afterward, I returned to the Moulin to pack my things.

Hearing a knock, I put down my folded clothes and
opened the door. Dusty was holding a plate with a slice of
the cake. We had ordered an English wedding fruitcake

covered in pale yellow and pink buttercream from the best patisserie in Avignon, topped with a Golden Gate bridge made from red hardened sugar.

"I thought you may want to try it," he said.

I took the plate and perched on the edge of the bed. "Without him, I'm afraid it won't taste half as good. I seem to have lost any appetite these last few days."

"He loved you, you know; he loved both of us. God knows he was always merry, but I haven't seen him so full of joy meeting someone new in a long time. It's funny; you pick up in a bar, you sleep with them, and you leave. I could have stayed home that night or could have spoken to someone else. It's so random. Never guessing the impact he would have on me. How he would change my life. Did you know we met again by sheer chance?"

"I thought you had known each other since the seventies."

"We only met for a single night. There were countless men. Endless days, weeks, and years ahead. When you're young, time never ends. We met again through mutual friends at a dinner in Montpellier ten years ago, after decades, and have been close ever since. It was such a shock seeing him. A kind of miracle. After the terrible times, the unimaginable times. What will you do now?"

"I'm going home to London, then Sam and I will move on. Honestly, I don't think stopping is in my blood."

"Why don't you both stay? To continue what he started."

After packing, I crossed the road but didn't go inside the house. I wandered to the back and knelt among the sage, oleander, and lantana, imagining a country of our own. What would the soil smell like? Queer earth and rock, without fudging or subterfuge. Nourished by the sun and rain and protected by a bitchy wind. A holy mountain of victory from which to watch the sunrise every morning together, without fail.

I stepped around the ancient machinery, looking up at the rail ties. After cutting the rope, we had put away the ladder. Thankfully, sparrows still swooped in and out of the building. A few had made their nests high in the iron joists, safe and sound. Flecks of rust dotted the floor at the spot, along with a single piece of straw, and dust hovered in the light from a crack in the stone. The moss would grow and the wood rot, but hopefully the birds would remain.

I took a bite of the fruitcake. It was delicious.

However Frank got up the ladder, he certainly never planned to climb down. While we know how he did it, I can only guess from what affliction Frank died: the lack of physical ability, or the inability to imagine a future with no past. Dusty thought he may have inadvertently done so under one of his disorientations, but I doubted in that state that someone could fashion a noose and climb a ladder. Still, Frank dying in his dreams in the 1980s was romantic. I knew he died as he lived, with flourish and agency.

Perhaps he just recognized the insufferable weight of survival, and all the days and days to come that he would bear on his already weary, stooped little shoulders, like an endless shadow of death passing over us.

RITORNELLO

There was no sign of the 3:00 a.m. ferry to Calais. I bought a ticket at the deserted booth inside the terminal. The genial lady behind the counter had a tight ash-blond perm, fuchsia nails like stalactites, and wore a sky-blue British Ferries nylon coat too big for her frame. She explained there was an hour delay in departure because of inclement weather on the English Channel.

I took a seat under the fluorescent lights at the far end of a line of orange fibreglass seats and opened my newspaper. Elton John had just married his German girlfriend, Renate Blauel, in St. Mark's church in Sydney. They were dressed in white and lilac, French kissing on the front page. I dry-heaved in the passenger restroom.

When I returned, beside me sat a slight, gamine girl, in her late teens like me, with a short but spiky pink mohawk, in a green leather jacket and baggy jeans. A pale yellow silk scarf was tied delicately around her neck and a small knap-sack and a violin case rested between her legs, with stickers for musicians like Nina Hagen and The Slits, and one that said WILLEM DE KOONING.

"It's a mean night for travel," I said.

"Grow up," she said.

In her lap was a small white bag of McDonald's french fries. I realized she was speaking to a group of men saun-tering past, laughing under their breath.

"Homophobes. Sorry, would you like a chip? There was nothing else open at this hour."

I took one of the small crispy ones. "Do you know those men?"

"From town. They live in the building behind me, and have felt more emboldened lately to spew epithets, but I'm a night owl and sleep in the day, so I don't have to see them often, or thankfully the town itself. If you think this place looks grim in the dark, you should see how vile it is at noon."

"I can imagine. Your mohawk is remarkable. How do you keep it standing up so well, may I ask?"

"Plaster of Paris. Dad had a sack lying around for flat repairs. I tried water and flour, but it disintegrated too easily. And then those yellow glue sticks. The school's art room had boxes of them, so I would nick a few at a time. They're handy for touch-ups, but not very practical for maintenance. Gypsum powder is brilliant."

We snort-laughed at the same time. Her eyes met mine.

"It was a jaunt to come down here from the station. Many detours and blocked roads," I said.

"The main street's closed due to burst sewage pipes," she said, "which makes the town smell like shite. Which, as you can see, is incredibly appropriate." She gestured like the prize girl on a game show.

"Is that why you're going to France?"

"That, and a million other reasons. I just feel better when I'm away. Does that make sense?"

"Perfect sense."

We chit-chatted. Her name was Manu, short for Manuela, and she was a visiting student in music studies at the National High Conservatory in Lyon, home for the weekend.

"It was quite a lot of money to attend, and my parents weren't in any position to help, so I followed my German girlfriend up north and worked at Blackpool Pleasure Beach for a few years as a seasonal fair worker. One afternoon in my first year, there was an accident on the ride I worked on called the Scrambler. Two people were killed when they were shot in the air after the safety bars failed, and a staff operating the gate lost his legs in the turbine."

"Were you hurt?"

"There was blood all over me, but it was someone else's."

She shifted in her seat and crossed her legs. "The whole place was a death trap. A woman operating the candy-floss maker had second-degree burns up her arms from exploding molten sugar. The unemployment and drug use up there was shocking, but this town isn't much better. Everything's boarded up, and the lights of Dover Castle are all on the blink. I was going to lose my shit if I didn't get out of here, so I kept working. My French is quite passable, but my year is over soon, and I don't know what I'll do afterward. I'd love to be a curator. I'm a born conservator and good at systematizing."

"My first boyfriend, Matthias, was German."

"Anneliese. Her family were Lutherans. She was very intense. Completely set in her ways at sixteen. Based on the average female life expectancy, I saw nothing changing for her over the next fifty-nine years, so we parted. I always knew I wanted to be an artist. I tried to break into the art world as a kid by signing up to be a life model. Nude and all that. But when I presented myself in the first class, they said they didn't employ minors. How was I to become a proper bohemian constantly confronting that kind of ageism?"

"It's very tiring."

"I had the most wonderful music teacher, so I learned the violin and fell in love with it. I still feel a heaviness when I return here, as if I was on trial. An eighteen-year-old going to live in France was a little suspect. I have an on-and-off girlfriend now in Lyon (it's a long story) pleading to move in together. We'll see. Maybe I've changed more than I realize. I may even be a different person. Hard to tell. I'm dreading taking the leap into co-habitation in case it doesn't work out. Still, I do love her. It's worth a try."

Manu stared at me for a long time, then nodded with satisfaction. "Where are you headed?"

"I'm going to Paris. I've just been released from hospital. After France, I'm heading north to Holland then hopefully on to West Germany, where he died, and where his parents still live. I'm hoping to find answers about his death."

She frowned and looked down, searching for something to say, but then the loudspeaker announced our boarding. We gathered our things, and she turned and hugged me tightly.

"Do you ever wonder how your choices change your circumstance? How it may have turned out completely different?"

"Often, yes. Enjoy the passage. I think Handel and Tchaikovsky are in excellent hands."

By the time the *St. Anselm* reached the open sea, the wind had subsided, and I tasted salt in the air. The rumble of the engines drowned out any sound of the waves. I moved to the edge of the rear platform, inhaling the fumes from the double stack of chimneys belching a trail of black smoke, and waved to Manu as she climbed the stairs some distance away.

My mind wandered back to Matthias, and his love of classical music and opera, how he taught me about Callas and the castrato Alessandro Moreschi, the first time he played me "Il dolce suono," the "mad scene" from *Lucia di Lammermoor*, in bed eating oranges in his Marble Arch flat, waiting for morning, when I saw the first strange purple lesions behind his ear and between his fingers, and he shrugged and told me it was nothing. The next evening, we attended a lecture on composition at the Royal Institution Theatre in Mayfair. Over a fireplace in the reception hall hung a large unattributed painting of early nineteenth-century Georgian gentlemen in formal waistcoats and pantaloons in the same theatre. On both sides of the chamber stood glass cases displaying the auspicious Victorian inventions unveiled there, including the first phonograph recording, the first still image from a calotype (the British version of the French daguerreotype), and the famous first moving image of a galloping horse using chronophotography. In the lecture, the composer explained the quick movements of Vivaldi's concertos were written in *ritornello* form, where a dominant theme is played at the start by the orchestra and returned to after every solo section, over and over. In the Spring concerto, the ritornellos were marked in the original sheet music by the word *tutti*, meaning everyone. Something made me look up. I studied the painting again, and the theatre had changed little in two hundred years. Only the people had been replaced.

Placing my left foot on the lower rail and both hands on the top, I leaned over to hear the foam escaping from somewhere deep in the ferry's belly. Whether from inhaling the acrid smoke or being overcome by my newfound freedom, or both, I felt dazed.

At first light I had a view of the horizon, a pearl-grey sky aflame with orange, and a fantasia of silvery clouds swirled above my head. And the sea, always the sea. On the platform below, a worker waited in grimy tan coveralls and a British Ferries hard hat, elbows on the railing, hands clasped, a line of thick mooring rope coiled at his feet like a sleeping python. From the deck above, I heard the opening chords of the Winter concerto of Vivaldi's *Four Seasons* being played on a violin, like the first few flakes descending from the old night, then the melody building, Manu's tremolo scratching out the rush of an ice storm.

ACKNOWLEDGEMENTS

To my mentor, Matthew J. Trafford, for watching over me on this journey, and to my readers — Rose Gowan, Mark Spencer, Laura Trunkey, Annie Game, Jerry Brennan, and Kellie Tatum — for their invaluable insights. Thank you to my residency hosts, Anne Jacquart at La Place Barcelona and Nicky Ginsberg at NG Art Creative Provence, as well as the Writers' Union of Canada. Special thanks to the entire team at Dundurn, including Janna Green, Shannon Whibbs, Laura Boyle, Eden Boudreau, Mylène Bouilly, Bex Lawlor, and especially my publisher and editor, Meghan Macdonald, for nurturing this project with such care and passion, and to Shaughnessy Bishop-Stall, Russell Smith, Mike Hoolboom, Catherine Bush, and Alan Mozes. Eternal thanks to Santosh, my partner and companion on the road always, and my own dear found family.

ABOUT THE AUTHOR

Ellis Scott was born in the U.K. and grew up in Canada. He has published nine stories in literary journals, including *The Iowa Review*, *Yolk*, and *The Fiddlehead*. His first short story was nominated for a 2020 Pushcart Prize. *Night Terminus* is his first novel.

JOSEPH COVINO JR

SAN FRANCISCO'S

FINEST:

GUNNING

FOR

THE

ZODIAC

EPIC PRESS

Published by:
Epic Press
PO Box 30108
Walnut Creek, CA 94598
JosephCovinoJr@gmail.com
First *Epic Press* Edition published 2012